THE OTHER WOMA

T0269843

"A fast-paced, no hold: real-estate agent who has just pulled off the deal of his career, but soon finds his life spiraling out of control. *The Other Woman* reads like the best of Gil Brewer's novels."
—Jeff Vorzimmer

"Stylistically understated, it springs to lyrical heights... And its intricate plot about a horny real estate agent who rediscovers the joys of marriage after a fling with a beckoning wanton pays rich dividends..."
—Marc Gerald, *Murder Plus*

"A sizable percentage of books from this era all have the same setup, but The Other Woman takes an abrupt left turn and becomes an honest-to-goodness murder mystery ... as good as they come."
—*Paperback Warrior*

Charles Burgess Bibliography

Novel:
Backfire (Australia, Phantom, 1959)
The Other Woman (Beacon, 1960)

Short Fiction:
"I'd Die for You" (*Manhunt*, Oct 1958)

True Crime as by Charles L. Burgess:
"Never Kill a Cop!" (*Complete Detective Cases*,
    Jan 1947)
"Case of the Buck-Happy Brunette"
    (*Revealing Detective Cases*, Aug 1949)
"A Killer with Women" (*Underworld Detective*,
    Dec 1951)
"Laughing Stranger from Dalton, Georgia"
    (*Official Detective Stories*, Feb 1956)
"Fat Man Blues" (*True Crime*, May 1956)

THE OTHER WOMAN

by Charles Burgess

Black Gat Books • Eureka California

THE OTHER WOMAN

Published by Black Gat Books
A division of Stark House Press
1315 H Street
Eureka, CA 95501, USA
griffinskye3@sbcglobal.net
www.starkhousepress.com

THE OTHER WOMAN

Originally published in paperback by Beacon Books, New York,
and copyright © 1960 Universal Publishing and Distributing
Corporation.

ISBN: 979-8-88601-108-1

Cover design by Jeff Vorzimmer, ¡caliente!design, Austin, Texas
Text design by Mark Shepard, shepgraphics.com
Cover art by Harry Barton

First Stark House Press/Black Gat Edition: July 2024

CHAPTER ONE

It was a telephone call that started the whole thing.

It came around ten o'clock. I was checking over some leases I'd just written up when the phone rang in the outer office and I heard Kathy pick up the receiver. When she stuck her head in the door a few moments later, her gray eyes were big as saucers.

"Mr. John Royal wants to speak to you," she whispered breathlessly.

It was my turn to be surprised. Royal was a big operator, one of the biggest on the west coast of Florida — certainly the biggest in Jellico.

"Okay, put him on," I said. My hand shook a little when I lifted the receiver. It isn't every day a big man like John Cameron Royal calls up a small real estate broker.

"Neil Cowan speaking," I said.

"This is John Royal, Mr. Cowan," said an authoritative voice. "I think you and I can do a little business."

"That's okay by me. What do you have in mind?"

"I understand you have Lake Chicopee land for sale."

"That's right."

"Fine. Can you come up to Peacock Hill this morning? I'd like to discuss that land."

I checked my watch. "I can be there in thirty minutes."

"I'll be expecting you."

After he hung up, I filed away the leases, then sat

down and tried to think. The Lake Chicopee property was owned by Sarah Graham, a crotchety old widow who lived on the other side of town. I took her folder from the cabinet and examined the data. She was asking a hundred and twenty thousand dollars for a strip of wooded land that extended from the lake to the highway, about forty acres in all. Three thousand dollars an acre was a fair price in my estimation, the way Jellico was spreading out. I wondered what John Royal wanted with the property. If he had another housing development in mind — he had erected several — he could not have picked a better spot.

I put the folder away, told Kathy where I was going and went out into the sunshine. My car was parked in the driveway next to the two-room bungalow that served as the office of Neil Cowan, Licensed Real Estate Broker. The sky was a cloudless blue and the slight breeze that came in off the gulf was hot and sticky. It was going to be another of those scorchers that hit the peninsula regularly during June, July and August. I lit a cigarette, started the engine, backed out of the driveway and headed for Peacock Hill, on the north end of town. The exclusive area around Curtis Circle and Arrowwood Road had been dubbed Peacock Hill by some imaginative citizen a long time ago, and the name had stuck.

As I wove through traffic, I wondered about Jellico's first family, the Royals. They had dominated the local scene ever since Jonathan Royal came to Jellico, shortly after the Civil War. It was rumored that the old boy had made his money by slave-trading, but by the time the story got around, nobody cared one way or the other. After Jonathan, a parade of Royals held sway over the town and its social and economic fortunes. Now there was only John Royal left. His wife, Annie May, had died while I was in the army, and the fact that she had borne him no children was the biggest disappointment in his life. Big shots have a mania for wanting someone to carry on their names, and John was no exception. Then, about a year ago, at the susceptible age of sixty, he had flitted off to New Orleans for the Mardi Gras and got himself hitched to a beautiful woman nearly thirty years his junior. Her name was Emmaline, and with her came her brother, Riley Martin.

Riley Martin's status on Peacock Hill puzzled me. As far as I could learn from the local gossips, he had done not a lick of work since coming to Jellico. Yet he drove a sporty red Porsche and always had money. This surprised everyone, for John Royal wasn't the kind of man who tolerated dead-beats.

I made a right turn on Belvedere Drive and swung into palm-lined Arrowwood Road. The Royal mansion, set well back from the road, was the last house on the block. I turned into a graveled driveway that ended under a trellised porte-cochere. Azaleas and hibiscus bloomed everywhere around the imposing two-story stucco. There was an atmosphere of quiet luxury about the place. To my appreciative lungs, even the air smelled of greenbacks. I got out, climbed the porch steps and pressed the ivory buzzer.

A light-colored Negress wearing a white cap and apron opened the door. She smiled pleasantly. "Mr. Cowan?" she asked. I nodded.

"Come this way, please. Mr. Royal is expecting you."

I removed my Panama and followed her along a cool, dim hall and into a large room. Two walls were completely lined with books and a number of comfortable-looking leather chairs were scattered about. A huge picture window looked out on an acre of neatly trimmed grass and shrubbery. The conditioned air was pine-scented.

There were two men in the room. John Royal, whom I recognized instantly from his newspaper pictures, was seated in a leather armchair. He was a mountain of a man, towering more than six feet three and weighing a good two hundred thirty pounds. His startling white hair was cut crew-style, and a smile split his florid face when he saw me.

"Come in, Mr. Cowan, come in!" he said heartily. He rose and clasped my hand firmly. "I like punctual men."

The second man had risen too. He was tall, with the slim hips and broad shoulders of a well-conditioned athlete. His dark hair, sharply etched features and pencil mustache made him look overly handsome. I guessed he was in his early thirties. Royal introduced him as Riley Martin and we shook hands. Then the big man waved us to chairs.

"Would you like something to drink?" he asked me.

"No, thanks."

"Then let's get down to business," he said. He crossed his legs and leaned back. "I'm interested in that Lake Chicopee property, Mr. Cowan."

"I gathered as much," I said.

Royal picked up a cigar from the ashstand next to

his chair and put a match to it. Exhaling deeply, he said, "I understand there are forty acres."

"That's right," I said. "It's six hundred sixty feet deep and two thousand six hundred forty feet along the lake."

"All level land?"

"Lots of pine and persimmon trees, but all level land."

"How much does old lady Graham want for it?"

"Three thousand an acre."

Royal took the cigar out of his mouth and whistled. "That's a lot of money," he said.

"Not the way Jellico is growing," I said. "I sold a lot out that way only last week for nearly four."

Royal's eyes narrowed. "Will she take less?"

"Do you know Mrs. Graham?" I asked.

"I've met her."

"Then you know how stubborn she can be."

Martin spoke for the first time, "Maybe you can talk her into taking less," he said in a deep, well-modulated voice.

"I can try," I said, "but I won't promise anything."

Martin leaned forward, elbows on knees. "If you could talk her down to a hundred grand, I'm sure John would split the difference with you. Ten thousand, plus your commission, is a mighty good inducement."

"I don't do business that way," I said stiffly. I decided that I did not like Riley Martin.

"Of course he doesn't," snapped Royal. He glared at the younger man, but Martin only leaned back and smiled. "Still, Mr. Cowan, I'd like you to talk to her.

Tell her I'll give her a hundred thousand for her land. If she needs the money bad enough — " he shrugged.

The sudden tap-tap of high heels cut my reply off, and I turned. A woman stood in the doorway, hands clasped demurely in front of her. John Royal's wife was tall and regally slender, with blonde hair that cascaded to her shoulders in shimmering waves. Her features were small and exquisitely chiseled and, while I couldn't be sure, a mocking smile seemed to lurk behind her steady blue eyes. Blue eyes in a woman have always had an electrically sensuous effect on me, but Emmaline Royal had more than her eyes to stir my senses. I said she was slender — This does not mean she lacked those special curves no mathematician can analyze. The severe black dress she wore clung to them lovingly. Just beneath the low, square neckline the points of her high, conical breasts brushed against the fabric, causing taut little tension lines to spring out against the fabric as she stirred. From her tiny waist the dress flared out again, stretching tightly across smoothly rounded hips. Her slim, elegantly shaped legs had the classic sheen of a polished marble statue, and the long, smooth calf muscles were those of a dancer. Mrs. Royal was easily the most beautiful woman I had ever seen.

"Come in, Emmaline," said Royal, standing. Martin and I followed suit. "I want you to meet Mr. Cowan."

Emmaline Royal came toward me slowly, her hand extended. "It's nice meeting you, Mr. Cowan," she said, her eyes regarding me unwaveringly. Her voice was low and vibrant. She walked erect, head held high.

Royal said, "Sit down, my dear. We were discussing

that land over by Lake Chicopee, and I have a feeling that Mr. Cowan is going to get Emmaline Acres for us."

"Emmaline Acres?" I asked.

Royal laughed. "A whim of mine, Mr. Cowan. I intend calling it after my wife when I get the property."

We discussed various facets of the deal and I could hear myself answer questions and even offer suggestions, but my voice seemed to come from someone else. I couldn't think straight, but fortunately my subconscious had come to my rescue and was saying the right things. Her beauty, the scent of her perfume, everything about her, had bowled me over. I had never felt this way about a woman before, not even my wife, Julie. And, God forgive me, the thought did not bother me.

Finally I sensed, rather than knew, that the interview was over. I got to my feet awkwardly.

"Well, that's about it," said Royal. The big man rose and clapped me on the back. "Have that talk with Mrs. Graham as soon as possible, Mr. Cowan. I'm anxious to get started."

I promised to do what I could, shook hands all around and left.

I went back to my car and drove out to Mrs. Graham's. The old lady lived in an antebellum house that must have been quite a showplace some seventy-five years ago. It was on a seldom-used dirt road about a mile north of what John Royal hoped would, one day, be Emmaline Acres. I didn't blame the old boy a bit. If I had something like her, I'd name a whole town after her. But you needed money to get a woman like

Emmaline Royal. A hell of a lot of it.

Mrs. Graham was glad to see me. She was a frayed, wizened-faced little woman who lived alone with her memories in that big house. A lot of folks didn't like her. They said she was too crabby. But she'd met Julie at a church bazaar, and somehow she had always afterward liked me. Maybe that was why she listed her property with me, rather than with one of Jellico's bigger firms.

I told her about John Royal's proposition, but she only waved a bony hand and laughed. "You go back and tell that old skinflint I want three thousand an acre for my land, not a penny less," she said. "He probably thinks I need the money real bad."

She had thought right, but I didn't tell her so. I didn't try to argue her down, either. She had her price and it was a fair one. Later, we had tea and cookies and chatted. It was past noon when I left.

Kathy was all ears when I got back to the office. She insisted on knowing how I had come out with John Royal, and I couldn't do a thing until I told her. She had been with me ever since she left high school. She was a good secretary, with just one fault — she talked too much.

Julie met me at the door that evening. When I saw the ecstatic look in her eyes, I knew that Kathy had phoned her the moment I left for Peacock Hill.

"Oh, Neil!" she exclaimed. "How did you make out? Is he going to buy the land? What did Mrs. Graham say?"

"Whoa, there!" I said, laughing. I picked her up and

whirled her around. "Take it easy, baby. One question at a time."

She looked cute in white cotton shorts and a halter, and for a moment I almost forgot the woman on Peacock Hill. Almost, but not quite.

Linda, our five-year-old daughter, came running in from the yard, a smear of dirt across her face. "Pick me up, Daddy!" she squealed. "Pick me up!"

I picked her up and whirled her around as I had Julie. It was a ritual we went through almost every night. I kissed her pink cheek and carried her into the living room. Julie followed, jabbering questions at me as I went.

I told her everything from the moment Royal called until I left Mrs. Graham's house. Everything, that is, except meeting Emmaline Royal. I had seen her only once, and already I was holding out on my wife.

Julie seemed disappointed when I finished.

"Suppose Mr. Royal won't pay her price?" she asked, biting her lip.

I put the squirming Linda down and she went scooting off into the yard. "He'll pay," I said confidently. "He's got his heart set on that land."

I knew what was bothering Julie — the six thousand commission I would get from the scale. It would be the largest I'd earned since I opened the office three years ago. The house on Maple Street was nice, but it was small. Only four rooms. Julie had hopes for a bigger house in a better neighborhood.

After dinner, we put Linda to bed and looked at television. It was nearly eleven when we shut it off and had our usual bedtime snack in the kitchen. All during the evening — and even while Julie and I were lying side by side in bed — Emmaline Royal's face kept floating around in the back of my mind. When Julie and I kissed good night, I was still thinking of her.

CHAPTER TWO

Mrs. Royal called early the next morning. I had just returned to the office after renting a beach bungalow to a couple of elderly tourists, when the phone rang. I recognized her voice immediately — I could feel my heart skip a beat.

"Mr. Cowan?"

"Yes, ma'am?"

A throaty chuckle came over the wire. "My, aren't we formal this morning!" she said. "Don't you know who this is?"

I knew who it was, all right. I'd know that voice anywhere. But I made it a question. "Mrs. Royal?"

"Of course, and I have a feeling you knew all the time." There was short pause, as if she were waiting for me to admit it. When I didn't, she asked, "Are you busy this morning?"

"Not very. What do you have in mind?"

"I'd like to see that pile of dirt John so facetiously calls Emmaline Acres. Will you take me?"

Would I take her? I'd take her to the moon if I had the proper launching platform. "I'll be glad to," I said. "Where shall I pick you up?"

"Let me pick you up," she suggested. "I'll be at your office at ten-thirty. You're on Longview Avenue, across the street from the Longview Apartments?"

"That's right. I'll be looking for you, Mrs. Royal."

My hands were perspiring when I hung up. I was glad Kathy was out of the office on a coffee break. I lit a cigarette and leaned back in the chair and thought of Emmaline Royal. Somehow her call had not surprised me. Call it intuition, hunch, or whatever tripe you believe in, but I had had a feeling that our first meeting would not be our last. Maybe I had seen it in her eyes when we looked at each other yesterday — my desire for her had been strong enough for her to have picked it up on her wave length.

She honked her horn at exactly ten-thirty. Kathy's eyes almost popped out of her head when she saw the sleek white Chrysler convertible sweep into the driveway. I shrugged into my coat and told her I'd be gone for an hour or so, that Mrs. Royal wanted to look over the lake property. For once Kathy was speechless, but her eyes got that know-it-all look teen-agers get when they think they're on to something.

Emmaline looked stunning in an off-the-shoulder linen dress with a wide leather belt and black, spike-heel pumps. She had a gaily colored kerchief tied around her head. As I slipped into the car, I wondered about those pumps. She evidently did not intend to do much walking when we got there.

She greeted me with that same Mona Lisa smile, and neither of us said anything until we were a couple of blocks from the office.

"Am I going in the right direction?" she asked.

"You've never been in the Lake Chicopee area, Mrs. Royal?"

She shrugged her suntanned shoulders. "I may have, but there are so many lakes around Jellico it's hard to tell which is which," she said. A pause, then: "Would you like to be my friend?"

I studied her profile, but it told me nothing. "I'd like it very much," I said.

"Then call me Emmaline. Only my enemies call me Mrs. Royal."

"I certainly don't want to be your enemy."

"That's better — Neil."

Lots of people called me by my first name, but none of them gave it quite that inflection, and it sent a thrill of pleasure up my back.

"How did you make out with Mrs. Graham?" she asked.

"Not too well. She insists on her price."

"Good for her!"

I grinned. "Whose side are you on, anyway?"

"I'm for her. We women have to stick together. Besides, John can afford to pay her price." She turned and looked at me. "Why haven't you called him?"

"I thought I'd try her again," I lied. "Turn right at the next corner."

She turned right on Sixth Street, then had to stop for a red light. "You're married, aren't you?"

"Yes."

"What's she like?"

"Julie? She's average, I suppose."

"Children?"

"A little girl, five years old. Her name's Linda."

"I'll bet she's cute."

"She is."

"And you and Julie are happy?"

I wondered what she was leading up to, if anything. "Yes, we're very happy," I said.

I wanted to say that I was very happy until yesterday

morning when she walked into my life, but I couldn't. It was hanging there, right on the tip of my tongue, but it wouldn't come out. But I think she guessed what I was trying to say, because she turned and stared into my eyes as if to say that she understood.

We didn't talk much until we came to Rosewood Street, which borders Lake Chicopee on the north side. I told her to turn right again, and she handled that big Chrysler like a sports car. We went along a dirt road for several hundred yards before I pointed to a narrow rutted path that led to the lake. She swung into it and stopped, a little way inside a tunnel of moss-draped persimmon trees. It was cool and restful in the shade, and Emmaline untied the scarf around her head and shook her blonde tresses loose.

"It's nice here," she said, sighing.

"You can see the lake through the trees."

She nodded. "It's easy to see why John wants this place. It's beautiful."

She sat quietly for several minutes, staring off into the trees. Then she turned and looked at me. The same small smile was on her lips, but her fathomless blue eyes were examining me as though I were something under a microscope. There was no sound but the rustling of the leaves. In a moment the situation was going to get out of hand. Believe me, I wanted it to, more than anything I'd ever wanted in my whole life.

"Do you want to walk around?" I asked inanely.

Her eyes continued to probe mine. "With these heels?" she said. She made my question sound as ridiculous as it was.

She reached toward me and pulled my face to hers. I was hoping for it, even expecting it, but its suddenness still surprised me. Her lips opened, soft and moist, and she kissed me. My arms went around her and I pulled her close to me as hard as I could. We strained together a moment, and then her tongue slipped between my lips. As it touched mine, I knew an electric thrill. My arms clasped her convulsively and a frantic, involuntary moan escaped both of us simultaneously. I could feel the pounding of her heart and the cushioning of her breasts against my chest. Time seemed to fly away on the scent of her perfume. It was a long, writhing, wild kiss, and when she finally withdrew her breathing was quick and ragged. Mine wasn't so steady, either.

"Should we have done that?" I asked. It came out hoarse, and sounded even sillier than the words themselves. It was my day for inanities.

Emmaline started to laugh, and I couldn't blame her. She didn't get very far with it, though, for this time I pulled her to me. I fastened my mouth hungrily on hers, and she hooked her fingers into my hair and gripped tightly. My hands moved on her back as our mouths devoured each other, and suddenly I realized she wasn't wearing a damned thing under that linen dress. After long, breathless moments she loosened her fingers and pulled her lips from my mouth. Her eyes were glazed, and she tilted her head to one side and turned them on me until they came back into focus.

She leaned her head against the cushion and ran a lacquered fingernail over my face. "You want me, don't you?" she whispered.

"You know I do." Sweat broke out between my shoulder blades and trickled down my back.

"Somebody's going to get hurt."

"I know."

"John could ruin us if he finds out."

"I know," I said again.

"You don't care?"

Our eyes met and held. "Of course I care — but I still want you."

She sat a long time, not saying anything but staring off into the trees. I just looked at her. She was the most beautiful woman I'd ever known. John Royal was a lucky man to have married a woman like her — but maybe his luck was running out. He had money, yet she had come to me. Money was important, but evidently it couldn't buy everything a woman like Emmaline needed.

She was looking at me again, studying me. "What about Julie?" she asked.

"What about her?"

"She won't like it. She might even leave you."

I didn't say anything. There didn't seem to be anything to say.

"It could break up your home."

I still didn't say anything. You can't argue against the irrefutable.

"Be honest, Neil. Do you want to go all the way?"

Daughter of Eve. Son of Adam.

I nodded. "All the way," I said.

"Where will it take us?"

"I don't know, or care."

Her eyes grew misty. "As long as we're together?" She put a soft hand over mine, running a fingernail gently up and down my wrist.

I kissed the tip of her nose. "As long as we're together," I said.

"Until we decide what to do, we'll have to be careful." "Yes."

She put her arms around my neck and her eyes got that funny look in them again. "Let's get in back, damn you!" she whispered huskily.

She kicked off the spike-heeled pumps and slid toward me. My left hand unlatched the door as my right went around her waist and pulled her the rest of the way across the seat. As I folded the backrest forward she squirmed around it, uttering a quick, silvery giggle as she made it into the back seat without getting out of the car.

I was right behind her. She sank down across the seat and my lips were on hers again, seeking hungrily. We kissed desperately, kissed until we were gasping for breath. Then, as our mouths separated, mine caressed her eyes, her nose, her ears, her throat. My hands seemed to move of their own volition to the zipper at the back of her neck, sliding it gently open and slipping the wide neckline of the dress down over her shoulders, my lips following eagerly.

As the glorious, quivering cones of her breasts sprang free of the linen, I gasped in delighted wonder. To their perfect, budlike pink tips, they were the same creamy, pale-golden tan as her shoulders — she had obviously been doing some very private sunbathing. Just a glimpse I caught, then both her slim hands locked tight in my hair and she crushed my face to her breast in the ancient gesture of woman lost in passion, her head thrown back, her lower lip caught between her teeth. From her throat came soft, frantic, whimpering moans.

My hands fumbled momentarily at her belt. It fell away, and she wriggled a little to help me work the dress over her hips. I reached blindly to drop it on the front seat while her hands were frantically unbuttoning my shirt. In the back seat now were only two vibrantly alive bodies, heaving wildly, lavishing, loving, under the cool arch of the persimmon trees. Then the obbligato of sighs and moans reached a crescendo and died away to slow, deep, shuddering breaths. At last we both lay perfectly still, locked so tight we might have been a single being.

Minutes later I stirred, raised myself slowly on my arms and gazed down at Emmaline Royal, feasting my eyes on the slim golden length of her. Her eyes opened, and she smiled meltingly up at me through the damp wisps of blonde hair fallen across her face. "Oh, my," she whispered. "Oh, my, how lovely!" She caught her lower lip between her teeth, raised one eyebrow slightly, lifted her hands to my elbows and tugged gently to bend them from their stiff position.

"Come back to me, darling," she said softly.

I let my arms relax and sank back down.

Much later, we went to the Harem Club on Highway 84. It was a small place, set half a mile from the road. The building was a one-story, sand-colored affair with a red tile roof and a green canopy that extended to the dirt road. A couple of cars were in the circular parking area. I'd never been there before and neither had Emmaline, which suited our purpose perfectly.

The inside was dim and cool. A long bar ran the length of the room, with a row of partitioned booths on one side. There was no harem motif that I could see. The few people at the bar paid us no attention as we found a red leather booth in the rear and ordered a couple of Bloody Marys. We didn't say anything until the waiter brought our drinks. Still wordlessly, we drank each other's health.

"Tell me about yourself, Neil," she said then.

"It's a dull story."

She placed an elbow on the table and cupped her chin in her palm. "Tell me anyway. Let's start with your age. How old are you?"

"Thirty-two."

"I'm two years older."

"What does that prove?"

She smiled. "Nothing, I suppose. Were you born in Jellico?"

I took a pack of cigarettes from my pocket, gave her one. "No," I said, exhaling. "I was born in a little town upstate, called Newdale. My folks moved here when I was a kid and it's been home ever since."

"Your parents are dead?"

"Yes. Dad was a conductor for the Atlantic Coast Line Railroad. He went first. Pneumonia. Mom lived on for a couple of years, but she was never the same. They loved each other very much."

Her eyes grew sad. "It's sad that everything we know must wither and die. Even love."

I sipped my drink. "I like to think that their love

didn't die, that they're together somewhere."

She studied me for several moments. "It's a nice thought, but you don't really believe it, do you?"

"Of course." I decided to switch to pleasanter channels.

"Tell me about yourself," I said.

She smiled. "I was born, grew up and here I am."

"What happened in between?"

"Lots of things," she said, her face sobering. "I was born on a little farm in the northwest corner of Mississippi. Father was a harsh man and drank too much. But liquor must have preserved his insides, because Mother went first. I was thirteen when he brought a woman home with him one night. They were dead drunk, both of them. It was my birthday and I was wearing my best dress — he had said we'd have a party when he came home. He had promised to bring me a cake, too, but he didn't. It was almost three o'clock when he finally showed up, and then he beat me because I wouldn't wait on Millie. That was the woman's name. I cried myself to sleep that night. God, how I cried. The next day I sneaked out of the house, and I've been on my own ever since. I've worked in carneys, night clubs, burlesque, stags. I even did a few bits in the movies." She smiled a little and shrugged. "It's not a pretty story."

"I wouldn't look back," I said gently. "Look where you are now."

"You mean John Royal?"

I nodded.

Her eyes flashed blue fire. "I hate him!"

Her vehemence startled me. "But why? You've hit

the jackpot. What more could a woman want?"

Her laugh was harsh. "You ask that — after what happened a little while ago?" she said.

When I didn't say anything, she said, "John Royal is a louse. There hasn't been a moment since we married that he hasn't thrown up to me that I am his property. He's a master at innuendo. He can, with a few well-chosen words, make me feel like some trollop he picked off the street." She puffed her cigarette furiously. "In some ways he reminds me of my father. God knows he's old enough. Only his way is right, only his judgment sound. He struts around that big house like he's God Almighty."

"Take it easy," I said. "He can't live forever."

I don't know why I said it. It just came out. But Emmaline didn't forget it. She reminded me of it later.

Her eyes got hard and shiny, and for a few moments I thought I was looking at another woman. She squashed out her cigarette and nodded. "You're right, Neil. He can't live forever."

The way she said it bothered me. I don't know why, because there was nothing in her tone to imply violence.

It was nearly two o'clock when Emmaline let me out in front of my office. We exchanged good afternoons as though nothing whatever had happened on the back seat of her car a few hours earlier. But a pact had been born under those persimmon trees. A pact that only one of us intended to keep.

Kathy managed to keep a straight face and tongue in cheek while she relayed some messages to me. I had to attend to two of them right away, and jumped into my Plymouth. An elderly couple on the west side of town wanted to sublet their apartment for sixty days while they attended their daughter's wedding up North. I jotted down the pertinent information and promised to do what I could. All the time they were showing me the place I was thinking about Emmaline and that back seat.

After the old couple, I went to see a man named Jennings who wanted to sell his antique shop. He was asking ten thousand. The store took in approximately five thousand a year after expenses, and I figured it would be a nice little business for a retired couple. I got him to sign a ninety-day listing contract which gave me exclusive selling rights to the business during that period. Such an agreement protected me so that even if he should sell it on his own, I'd still get my commission.

It was almost five o'clock when I got back to the office. Kathy had her bag on the desk and was fixing her face. I had kept her overtime — she usually left around four-thirty.

"Sorry I'm late," I said. I tossed the papers and notes from the two calls into the metal basket on her desk. "You can type this up tomorrow."

She got up and started for the door. Halfway there she turned and said, "Mr. Cowan?"

"Yes, Kathy?"

"Mrs. Royal is very pretty, isn't she?"

So that was what was bugging her. "Yes, she's very pretty."

She swallowed hard and shifted her weight from one ballet-slippered foot to the other. "You won't become involved, will you, Mr. Cowan?"

I shook my head and smiled. "No, Kathy, I won't become involved," I said. "Now run along. I'll see you tomorrow."

She smiled uncertainly and left, closing the screen door quietly behind her.

I had lied to her. I was involved. Right up to my neck.

Julie was her usual effervescent self when I got home. Linda was in the back yard playing with the Peterson children next door, and I could hear their squeals of delight as I read the Jellico *Sentinel*.

I was helping Julie with the dinner dishes when she finally asked me how I had made out with John Royal.

"I haven't phoned him yet," I said.

"Didn't he ask you to get in touch with him right away?" she asked, handing me a wet dish.

I dried it. "I don't like to rush things, Julie."

She frowned, puzzled by the complexities of business. "Maybe you're right, Neil," she said. "But I kept hoping all day that you'd told him and that he had accepted her price."

"He will," I said.

Typical husband-and-wife scene? Of course. But there was something missing. I couldn't put my finger on it, but Julie and even little Linda seemed somehow strangers to me. It was as if some unknown force were crowding them back into my subconscious — as if they were no longer as important to me as they had once been.

I hated myself for feeling this way. Emmaline was

right. She had said that somebody was going to be hurt. Forty-eight hours ago I would have strangled anyone who dared come between my family and me. Now it had happened.

I didn't sleep much that night.

CHAPTER THREE

John Royal was in an expansive mood when I drove up to Peacock Hill the next morning to tell him about my futile talk with Mrs. Graham. He had called shortly after I arrived at the office and requested my presence right away. I found him on the back terrace, trimming some viburnum hedges with an electric clipper. He was wearing a pair of faded overalls and cotton work gloves, and the inevitable cigar was in his mouth.

He turned and grinned when he saw me. "No luck with the old battle-axe, eh?" he chuckled.

"No luck," I said. "She's a very stubborn woman, Mr. Royal."

He chuckled again, pulled the cigar from his mouth and shook his head. "Don't I know it," he said. "Sarah's quite a character. Did you know that my dad used to court her?"

I smiled. "That right?"

Royal nodded and resumed his trimming. The clipper made a humming sound. "I haven't spoken to Sarah since Dad's funeral, more than twenty years ago," he said. "She got mad because I wouldn't put her in the first car in the procession. She thought she deserved special consideration because she knew Dad before Mother did."

I looked around while he was talking, but Emmaline wasn't in sight. I was hoping to catch a glimpse of her before I left.

"Yeah," he went on. "Sarah was a hellwinder in her day. My dad told me they had some swell times. He said they almost got hitched a couple of times, but she was too much for him."

Royal snipped a few more branches off the hedge and then crouched, surveying it carefully.

"Well, I guess she's got me over a barrel," he said, straightening. He snapped the switch, shutting off the power. "I want that land, Mr. Cowan. So I guess you'd better draw up the papers. At her price."

"I checked the abstract before I came up here," I said. "Mrs. Graham hasn't bothered to keep it up to date. I know there is nothing wrong, but the title should be searched before you go any further."

He nodded. "Do what you think best," he said. "Would you like a deposit?"

"It's customary."

Royal placed the clippers on the ground and removed his gloves. "Okay, let's go in the house. I'll give you a check."

He took me to a small room on the ground floor. There were several rifles hung neatly on the wall. I recognized a bolt-action Mossberg 144 model and an H and R slide-action 422. A number of trophies were scattered about the room, on the mantelpiece and the teakwood wedge tables. It was a comfortable room — a man's room.

"Grab a chair," he said, waving a huge arm. He went behind a small desk, took a checkbook from one of the drawers and began writing. When he was finished, he tore it from the book and pushed it across the desk.

It was for five thousand dollars.

"That enough, Mr. Cowan?"

I said yes and put the check in my wallet. "What type of homes do you figure on putting up?" I asked.

Royal crushed out his cigar in an ashtray and folded his hands behind his head. "I think the twelve to fifteen thousand dollar models would be best for that area," he said. "I'll have the usual fifty-foot right-of-way for the streets, and sixty-foot lots. That should allow me to build about four houses to the acre, or about a hundred and sixty homes."

"Not bad. It's a fine location and they should move fast."

Royal nodded. "That's how I feel, too." He gazed at me thoughtfully for several seconds. "How about handling them for me when we get started?"

"You mean sell them for you?" I asked, surprised.

"Why not? You have an excellent reputation in town, and you're in the real estate business."

"I'd consider it a privilege — and a great opportunity."

It was the chance of a lifetime. My brain whirled. He would have had no trouble selling them himself, yet he had given the business to me. The man was throwing a small fortune in my lap, and I was repaying him by fooling around with his wife. The thought sickened me.

But I still wanted her.

She phoned me twice during the next two days. We met each night under the persimmon trees, and later we had something to eat at some out-of-the-way spot where neither of us was known. I was completely enslaved by now, and if her actions were any criterion she went for me, too. There was trouble ahead, but I was too blind to see it. I was on cloud eleven, floating high, wide and handsome.

Meanwhile, there were things to be done in my real estate business. I had one of the title companies search the Lake Chicopee property. As I had expected, it came through free and clear of any encumbrances. While they were bringing the abstract up to date, I got the deed from Mrs. Graham. By Monday morning the deal was closed.

I didn't see Emmaline over the weekend, and I never thought forty-eight hours could be so long. She was on my mind constantly. I walked around the house in a daze. Several times I caught Julie looking at me with wondering eyes. I knew I'd have to snap out of it. Julie was trusting, but she was sharp, and she knew me like a book.

Emmaline phoned on Monday afternoon while Kathy was on her lunch hour. She was in excellent spirits.

"John has left for Tampa on business," she said, "and won't be back for two days at least. How about tonight?"

"You've got a date," I said. "Same place?"

"It'll have to be, Neil. And I think we'd better stop going to these spots around Jellico afterwards. Too many people know my face."

She was right, of course. Jellico was a good-sized town, but the Royals had had their pictures in the paper so often that they were almost as well-known as Governor Collins.

I blew her a kiss and hung up. It was only one-fifteen, which meant I had nearly eight hours of waiting ahead of me. Just thinking about seeing her again made me restless. I lit a cigarette and strolled over to the window. There was a row of three-story apartment houses on the next street, and the back yards were full of newly washed laundry. I was still thinking about Emmaline when the screen door to the street slammed. It was too early for Kathy to return from her lunch, and I turned, expecting a customer.

It was Riley Martin.

He looked like an *Esquire* ad in a checkered white sports shirt, tan gabardine slacks and white-and-tan shoes. There was a thin smile on his handsome face.

I sat behind the desk and motioned him to a chair. He shook his head and it was only then I saw there was something wrong. His eyes were pinpoints of carefully controlled anger.

"What can I do for you?" I asked, squashing out my cigarette.

"Will you answer a few questions?"

"If I can."

"How old are you, Mr. Cowan?"

His sister had asked me the same question. Curiosity must run in the family. "I'm thirty-two," I said.

"How tall?"

"Six-one."

"And your weight?"

"It varies. Right now it's one eighty-five." I lit a cigarette and exhaled deeply. "I suppose you have a good reason for asking these questions?"

He leaned against the door frame like an indolent

panther. "Yes, Mr. Cowan. A very good reason. You see, I'm the same age as you, also the same height. I have a couple of pounds on you, but that shouldn't handicap you too much."

"Are we having some kind of competition?"

"I hope not, Mr. Cowan. For your sake." He walked to the desk, placed his hands very carefully on its smooth surface and leaned forward. "I just wanted to get the statistics straight before I pushed in that good-looking face of yours." His voice was stiff with emotion.

I studied his eyes. He wasn't bluffing.

"Mind telling me what this is all about?" I asked.

He didn't move a muscle. "No, I don't mind telling you. I want you to stay away from my sister."

It caught me by surprise. We'd been together only a half-dozen times, and already the word had gotten around.

"I don't know what you're talking about," I said.

"Let's stop kidding one another, shall we? You were at the Harem Club and also the Tic-Tac-Toe with her. I've got witnesses."

I could feel my temper slipping. "So what if we were having a drink?" I retorted. "Mrs. Royal happens to be over twenty-one."

"And she also happens to be married to John Royal," Martin snapped. "I don't want anything to happen to that marriage. Do I make myself clear?"

"You're beginning to." I stood up and our eyes held. "If Mr. Royal should find out, the gravy train would be over for you. He'll divorce your sister and throw you out on your big fat ass."

Martin straightened, fluffed an imaginary piece of

lint off his arm. "That is correct, Mr. Cowan," he said.
"I have no intention of letting my hot-pants sister
spoil everything for me. I've got a good setup on
Peacock Hill and I intend to keep it that way. If I hear
that she's still seeing you, I'm coming after you.
Remember that, lover-boy."

"I'm scared stiff," I said evenly. "Go on, get lost."

He stopped at the door and turned. "Remember what
I said, Cowan."

"Get out before I throw you out."

He smiled and ran his eyes over me slowly. "That
would be quite a job, believe me," he said.

He wasn't kidding. It would be quite a job, especially
since lifting a telephone receiver was the heaviest
exercise I'd taken since my army days.

Despite Martin's warning, I met Emmaline that
night as usual. She looked lovely in a black satin dress
with a belled skirt. I told her about her brother's visit
and it upset her.

"We've got to be more careful, Neil," she said. Her
eyes probed the darkness around us furtively. "Riley's
my own brother, but he's no good. Work has always
been a dirty word to him, and I doubt if he's ever
earned an honest dollar in his life. When he's mad,
he's a mean, vindictive person."

"Why does Royal put up with him?"

Emmaline shrugged. "Only because of me. They've
had several tiffs, and once John threatened to throw
him out of the house. I had a time patching that one
up."

She laid her head on my shoulder, and we sat that

way for a long time, saying nothing and being content with each other's company. But every little sound worried her and I could feel her body stiffen with fright. I kept telling her not to worry, that if Martin knew where we were, he'd have shown up by now.

But nothing I said reassured her. Even when we climbed in back, her fear was like an invisible wall between us.

We met twice during the next few days, each time at our spot in the woods. But even that haven would soon be lost to us, for the bulldozers and tractors were already at work, pulling down the trees and grading the land. I'd heard no more from Riley Martin, so I figured that my warning to Emmaline to make sure she wasn't followed must have paid off.

If Julie was suspicious about my frequent nocturnal absences, she didn't show it. I explained that some of my clients couldn't be seen during working hours and could only be reached at night. The hardest part was lying to her, because every time she looked at me, the love and trust in her eyes were like a knife in my heart.

I was a heel and there was nothing I wanted to do about it. Good or bad, Emmaline was in my blood. Loving her was like sitting atop a volcano.

Julie was overjoyed when the six-thousand-dollar commission from the Lake Chicopee deal went into the bank. And her eyes lighted up when I told her about Royal's offer to let me handle the selling job out at Emmaline Acres.

"Neil, we'll have enough to build in Highland Shores," she exclaimed excitedly.

Highland Shores was a slightly better than middle-class development on the southern outskirts of the city. It was comparatively new and except for Peacock Hill, it was the swankiest section in the city.

"Sure, we will," I said. But my heart didn't share her enthusiasm. I felt happy and miserable at the same time. Happy because I had Emmaline and sad because I was losing Julie. And, when the time came, I would lose Linda, too.

It was a hell of a lot to give up for a woman.

Emmaline telephoned on Thursday. I hadn't seen her since Monday night, and I was going nuts wondering about her. I was worried, but her lilting voice reassured me.

"How's my lover-boy?" she teased.

Martin had used the same words, but from her I didn't mind. "I'm fine. What can I do for you, madam?"

She laughed. "Is that the way you talk to your women customers?"

"Only those I meet socially."

"Darling, I've only got a minute. John has a meeting tonight at the Civic Center. Are you available?"

I grinned into the receiver. "I'll think about it."

"You'd better be there."

"I'll be there."

The hours dragged, as they always did when I was about to see her. I should have been scared, I suppose. Her brother was gunning for me and my home, my business, everything I'd built up was going to tumble around me if I kept seeing her. But I couldn't stop. It was like going down a steep hill at terrific speed and finding out that your brakes won't hold.

She was there when I got to our favorite rendezvous. I parked the Plymouth behind the Chrysler, got out and slid into the seat beside her. She floated into my arms as though everything was rehearsed. Only this was no play — it was unbelievably real.

When she finally pulled away, she murmured in my ear, "Miss me?"

"I won't even answer that one."

She smiled and ran her hand caressingly across my face. "Why?"

"Because it's the silliest question I've heard all day."

She tweaked my nose in pretended anger. "So my questions are silly, are they?"

I kissed her gently. "That kind is."

It was a quiet night. There was a full moon, and a gentle breeze blew from the lake. In the distance we could see the darkened hulk of a big steam shovel through the trees. In another week our trysting place would be no more. A feeling of sadness came over me.

"You're very quiet, Neil," she said, divining my mood. "Is anything wrong?"

I nodded to the big shovel. "They're taking our rendezvous away from us, Emmaline," I said.

"We'll find another place."

Her face was clear and lovely, and little flecks of moonbeam glinted in her hair. She was quiet for a few moments.

"You're not sorry about this — about us?" Her eyes searched mine for the answer before I could speak.

"No, I'm not sorry. I'd do it all over again. I guess I'm just sentimental about this place."

"You remind me of a fellow I used to know in Los

Angeles," she said, staring off into the darkness. "He used to cry when he saw anything sad, in the movies, on television, anything. I tried to chide him out of it, but it didn't do any good. He was just a softie."

"Is that what you think I am, a softie?"

She reached for my hand and held it. "I'm afraid you are, darling. I love you all the more for it. But because you are what you are, I don't think we'll ever be free to have each other."

"You mean Julie?"

"And Linda."

I tilted her head back and kissed her on the lips. "I can walk out any time," I said. "Can you?"

She weighed the question carefully before answering. "You want the truth, Neil?"

"The truth."

She shook her head. "I can't just walk out of John Royal's life," she said huskily. "Oh, it isn't because I have any feeling for him. That went out the window a long time ago." Her body and voice were tense. "Let's face it, Neil. You're in love with a mercenary woman. Why else would I marry a man old enough to be my father?"

I wasn't shocked. I should have been, I suppose. But the thought of her marrying Royal for his money had occurred to me from the start.

The thought of her in love with her husband was unendurable.

"You can't have me and his money," I said.

She looked up and her eyes found mine. "But I can," she whispered. "I can be rich and so can you."

I shook my head. "That's nonsense, Emmaline.

There's only one way that can — "

"Yes," she said quickly. "I know, and you know it, too. John has to die."

My body went numb. There were words of protest on my lips, but they remained frozen.

"You said yourself that he can't live forever," she said, pushing her body close to mine. "What's the difference whether it's now or ten years from now? Time to a man past a certain age means nothing. John's had enough out of life — out of me."

I was horrified. Stealing a man's wife was bad enough, though it was being done every day. But murder! That was being done every day, too, but not by people like me.

"Neil, are you listening to me?" She took my face in her hands and stared hard into my eyes. "We're young. We have a whole lifetime before us, and we'll have everything we'll ever want. Paris, Rome, the Riviera. Think of it, Neil!"

The numbness went out of my body. I grabbed her wrists and pulled them away from my face. "I am thinking of it," I said. I tried to keep the disillusionment from showing in my face, in my voice. "I love you more than anyone or anything in my life. I'll go all the way for you, no matter what. Except murder. That's one thing I won't do, not even for you."

She slumped over the steering wheel and covered her face with her hands. She began to cry, softly at first, then with such intensity that her shoulders shook. I lit a cigarette and sat there, strangely unmoved. As far as I was concerned, it was all over between us. You can give a woman just so much love and no more, and I'd loved Emmaline Royal just short of the limit. Murder.

After a long while she wiped her eyes and looked at me. "I'm a wicked woman, Neil," she said.

"Let's not talk about it."

A whippoorwill called in one of the trees. The lingering wail of a siren could be heard in the distance.

"Light me a cigarette, Neil," she said.

I lit one for her from mine and gave it to her. Then I crushed mine out in the ashtray.

"You're mad at me, aren't you?"

"I'm not mad at you," I said. "Let's say I'm disappointed." I turned and faced her. "Look, I'm far from a saint, I've done some lousy things in my life, but I don't know where you got the idea I'd kill for you. Besides, John Royal has been wonderful to me."

She laughed. It was a dry, cackling laugh, tinged with hysteria. "You have quite a code of morals, Neil," she said harshly. "You're grateful to him for favors rendered, yet you have no qualms about climbing aboard his wife."

It was true, and it hurt like hell. I slid out of the car and closed the door quietly.

"Maybe so," I admitted. "But that's the way things are. I'm sorry, Emmaline."

I'm sorry, Emmaline. I didn't know which hurt more — saying goodbye or finding out where she thought our love should lead.

The house was dark when I got home. Julie was asleep, but she had left the automatic percolator on and there was a piece of apple pie in the refrigerator. I downed the coffee and thought again about

Emmaline, and for a moment I was back in the car
with her.

It would have been easy to have said, Yes, Emmaline,
I'll help you get rid of your husband. It'll be risky, but
after it's all over we'll have each other forever. And
don't forget the money. No, don't forget the goddamn
money. That's the most important part of all . . .

Easy, sure, I shook myself.

I'd been the biggest kind of fool to think I could find
happiness without Julie and Linda. I washed and
dried the cup and saucer, turned out the lights and
went to bed.

During the night, Julie tossed in her sleep and put
her arm around me. It felt warm and comforting. I
was where I belonged. But my troubles were just
beginning.

CHAPTER FOUR

That Sunday I took Julie and Linda out to Highland Shores. Julie was anxious to find a site for our new home, and her enthusiasm was infectious. We found several good lots for sale, but they were only seventy-five feet wide, and she insisted on having one that was at least a hundred. For a while it didn't look as though we were going to find what we wanted. Then we came across a lot on the west side of the lake. It was plenty large, one twenty-five by three hundred.

According to the sign, Bob Jamieson was handling it. Since Bob was my legal adviser, I knew I could get it fairly reasonably. Linda scooted around the lot like a puppy, asking innumerable questions, some of which would have stumped a Supreme Court justice.

Julie stood off to one side, arms akimbo, and surveyed the land with a critical eye. "What do you think, Neil?" she asked.

I could see she was so happy she was ready to burst. "It's good, level land," I said. "And it's far enough from the lake to keep Miss You-Know-Who out of trouble."

"Do you think it's wide enough for a ranch-type house?"

"I think so. The average ranch-type runs to about seventy-five to eighty-foot front. That would leave us plenty of room on either side."

When we got back to the house I called Jamie at his home and asked him about the lot. He quoted a fair price and I promised to be in his office in the morning with a deposit.

After checking with Kathy the next morning, I drove to Jamie's office in the Westminster Building and gave him a deposit on the Highland Shores property. He promised a clear deed in a couple of days and I went back to my office.

Now that I had decided not to see Emmaline any more, I felt curiously free, as if a load had rolled from my shoulders, though I was far from happy. She was not the kind of woman you could forget easily. But the way I figured it, I was lucky. I had escaped a dangerous situation unscratched and unscarred. Or so I thought.

I was getting ready to leave for lunch when the phone rang. The man's voice was unfamiliar, and he spoke with a pronounced Spanish accent.

"Meester Cowan?"

"Speaking."

"You are acquainted with Señor Royal, no?" There were muted voices in the background. And music. Jukebox music.

"Yes, I know Mr. Royal."

"He wishes the pleasure of your company this evening at his home. Say, around nine o'clock?"

"Who is this?" I asked.

"My name is Raúl Antonio Lopez, *señor*. I am a very good friend of Señor Royal's."

"Why doesn't he call himself?"

"A thousand pardons, Señor Cowan. But Señor Royal is in conference and he asked me to do him this one small favor. Will you come?"

Why not? I thought. I had nothing to lose. The *affaire d'amour* was over. Finished. Nothing, I was determined, could revive it.

"I'll be there at nine," I said.

I wondered what Royal wanted. The deal for the Lake Chicopee land was settled, and there were no loose ends that I knew of. I was certain that the invitation had nothing to do with my seeing Emmaline, because I was sure Riley Martin would not jeopardize his lush existence by telling Royal. Also, Royal would hardly invite me to his home to discuss his wife's love affairs. Or would he? It was all very puzzling.

I was kept busy during the morning showing the antique shop to a couple of prospective buyers from Michigan. They liked the price and thought the yearly income was sufficient, but were hesitant about investing their savings in a business they knew nothing about. They finally promised to think it over and let me know. It was nearly one o'clock when I let them out in front of their hotel, and I went to lunch.

The Patio Club is located just off Main Street in Jellico's business district. It's a quiet, dimly lit spot where they play organ music and serve the most delicious planked steak in the South. I eat there when my finances permit, and with the Lake Chicopee deal in the bag, I figured I could fly a little.

The place was well filled, but I was able to find a secluded spot in the rear. After I'd ordered, I wondered again about Raúl Antonio Lopez. Who was he, and what was he doing on Peacock Hill? Emmaline had never mentioned him. I was still trying to find the answers when someone slipped into the booth beside me.

It was Emmaline.

On the surface she looked different. A chastened Emmaline. There was an uncertain smile on her lips as she laid her bag and gloves on the table. She reached for my hand and squeezed it. Her fingers were like ice.

"Please don't send me away, Neil," she whispered in a pleading voice. "I had to see you!"

All we had been to each other before that last meeting came back to me when I saw her. My eyes feasted on her — and yet I didn't want any part of her. *Who do you think you're kidding, Neil Cowan?* She was something I wanted — and she was poison.

"How did you know I was here?" I asked finally.

"I followed you."

I offered her a cigarette. She took it and I lit it for her, and then I lit one for myself. A hidden organ was playing a soft number I didn't recognize.

"I must see you tonight, Neil," she said. There was urgency in her voice — whatever she had in mind was important, at least to her.

"Why?"

She shook her head. "We can't talk here. Please, Neil?"

I was trying my damnedest to appear unmoved. "I thought we settled everything the other night?"

A sheen of tears filmed her eyes. "I was a fool," she said bitterly. "I was so desperate I didn't know what I was saying."

"It's no good, Emmaline," I said. I studied the lighted end of my cigarette. It was difficult, but this was something I had to say: "We've been acting like a couple of adolescents. But we know better now. At least I do."

Her hand squeezed mine again and the shock went all through my body. "Please, Neil. Just this once. If you still don't want to see me after tonight, I'll never bother you again."

"What time tonight?" I hadn't meant to say it.

She leaned her head back on the cushion and rewarded me with a beautiful smile. "Thank you, Neil! I knew you wouldn't let me down."

"What time tonight?" I asked again.

"Nine o'clock. Same place as before."

I remembered Señor Lopez. "I have an appointment with your husband at nine," I said. "I'm sorry."

She stiffened and looked at me, puzzled. "You're seeing John tonight?"

"Yes. A man with a Spanish accent called me this morning and said that Mr. Royal wanted to see me at nine. It must be about that Lake Chicopee deal."

Something like fear leaped into her eyes. "Neil, my husband doesn't know anybody with a Spanish accent!" she exclaimed in a low voice.

I frowned. "He said his name was Raúl Lopez. He also claims to be a very good friend of your husband's."

"I tell you John doesn't know any such man!" She looked around her furtively. "Neil, it's a trap!"

Her seriousness made me laugh. "Don't be melodramatic. You make it sound like a cloak-and-dagger movie."

She grabbed my hand again, and I could feel the tension building up inside her. "Don't go up to Peacock Hill tonight. Please, for my sake."

My lunch arrived at this moment, and I asked her whether she wanted anything. She settled for a glass of sherry.

"I'm not being melodramatic," she said after the waiter had left. "Neither John nor I know a man named Raúl Lopez. He's an impostor, whoever he is."

I was beginning to think she might have something. I had heard voices and juke-box music when he called, which meant he hadn't called from Peacock Hill.

I shook my head, puzzled. "Are you sure you're not being too suspicious — just because — well, we share the same guilt?"

"I don't know." She took a good gulp of sherry. "But I do know this — you've got to be careful. We both have to."

That much was obvious.

She squeezed my hand. "Promise you won't see John tonight? There's something important I've got to tell you."

I thought about it, then said, "All right."

Her eyes mirrored her relief. "Thank you, Neil." She finished her drink. "I'll see you tonight? Same place?"

"At nine," I said.

She slipped on her gloves, picked up her bag and eased out of the booth. She gave me a grateful smile and left. I watched her weave her way among the tables, and couldn't help thinking what a physically glorious woman she was.

The afternoon was taken up with attending to the myriad details of a fifty-acre orange grove that I managed for a couple who spent their summers in New England. The monetary return for such work isn't nearly worth the energy expended, but in real estate you soon learn to make it while you can. There are a lot of dry spells in this business. Right now I was riding a run of luck, but I knew it couldn't last.

After dinner I told Julie I had to go out on a call. She walked with me to the car and kissed me goodbye. It was a little too early for my rendezvous, so I decided to kill a little time by driving out to Highland Shores and looking at the lot. Julie's lot. When I got there I saw that Jamie had taken the sign down and put a SOLD sign up in its place.

I switched off the engine and looked at the lot and the surrounding landscape. It was quiet here by the lake, and I knew that Julie and I were making no mistake in building here. After a few minutes, I started the car again and headed back to town. It was dusk by now, and lights were springing up all over town.

I liked Jellico. It was a medium-sized, cleanly run town of about forty-five thousand. A five-man city commission was elected every two years. Nearly half the residents are transplanted snowbirds from the north, who've made their adjustment to our ways and the result was a cooperative, well-adjusted community. But Jellico was growing a mite too fast to suit me. It would never be another St. Petersburg or Tampa, but in time it would have small-city stature.

It was exactly nine o'clock when I swung into the narrow dirt path that led to our trysting place under the persimmon trees. Emmaline's Chrysler was nowhere in sight as I eased the Plymouth far enough into the woods to allow her room to park behind me. I lit a cigarette and waited.

The steam shovels and bulldozers were much closer now, and I knew that it would be only a day or two before the entire forty acres would be devoid of woods. Huge piles of dead trees littered the ground and the smell of wood-smoke was strong on the night air.

The minutes ticked away slowly. I was getting impatient. I turned on the radio, listened to some music for a few moments, then switched it off. She had never been this late before, and I couldn't help wondering whether my Spanish caller had anything to do with her delay. I suddenly realized I hadn't the slightest idea of what was going on — why the unknown caller had wanted me on Peacock Hill, or what Emmaline had in mind when she asked to meet me tonight.

When she didn't show by ten o'clock, I was sure she wasn't coming. I was puzzled. Something was happening I didn't know about and Emmaline's unease at lunch was making a belated impression on me. I drove back to town, parked across the street from the City Hall and went into a drug store. I meant to call her, but now that I was in the telephone booth with the dime in my hand, it didn't seem like a good idea.

Finally I decided against making the call and went out. There were a few people on the street. Walking toward my car, I saw a familiar figure striding towards me. It was Riley Martin. He saw me and smiled.

"Well, well. If it isn't lover-boy," he said, grinning. "I'm glad you took my advice."

"I'm glad you're glad," I said shortly.

I started to walk around him, but he moved into my

path. "What's your hurry, Mr. Cowan? How about a drink?"

"I drink only with my friends."

His grin widened and I put my hands in my pockets to keep from punching him in the nose.

"You didn't finish the sentence, Mr. Cowan," he said. "You should have said, 'I drink only with my friends and with married women.'"

I looked at him steadily. "Are you looking for trouble?"

His smile was disarming. "Of course not. Only fools fight in public, and I know now that you're no fool."

"Then listen carefully," I said. "I'm going to my car, but if you stand in my way again, you're going to be a very busy guy during the next few minutes."

He clicked his heels like a Prussian officer and bowed from the waist. "In your condition, that's about all you'd last," he said mockingly. "A few minutes."

I disregarded his taunt, got into my car and drove off. Heading toward Maple Street, I had to agree with him on one point. A few minutes would be about my limit in a rough house.

Julie was having her bedtime cup of coffee when I got home. She fixed me a cup and then she told me about the wonderful TV programs I'd missed.

"The one I liked best was *Peace Officer*. There was this man, and he was going with this woman. He didn't know she was married, so when some campers found his body in the woods, the sheriff figured her husband got wise and killed him ..."

Julie went on, but I didn't hear her. Except for the murder, the story hit so close that I was startled. Emotionally, I was familiar with every nuance of the situation and plot. I studied her over the cup and wondered whether my smart little wife didn't know a lot more than I gave her credit for. But she was only explaining a television play.

". . . Anyway, the sheriff got to work on the case and pretty soon he found a flaw in the husband's alibi," she went on. "After that it didn't take him long to prove that he had killed the boy friend. I think Peter Hennings does a grand job as the sheriff."

I had seen the program many times and I thought Hennings was good, too.

"I dropped by our lot tonight," I said. "Jamie took the sign down."

"That's wonderful," said Julie, her eyes shining. "What do we do now?"

"Get some plans and pick one we like. I saw a book the other day that showed a hundred different house plans. I'll pick one up tomorrow."

It was some time before I got to sleep. I kept thinking about the guy with the Spanish accent. And Emmaline. What did she want to see me about, and why hadn't she shown up?

The Tampa *Tribune* was lying on the lawn when I left for my office the next morning. As always, it was rolled up and tied with a string. As on every other morning, I gave it to Julie, kissed her and drove off.

The minute I got to the office I knew that something was wrong. Kathy was sitting behind her desk and staring at me with frightened eyes.

"What's the matter?" I asked.

"Have you seen the paper this morning, Mr. Cowan?" she asked, in a scared little voice.

"Not yet. Why?"

She opened a drawer and took out a folded copy of the *Tribune*. "Take a look," she said.

I didn't unfold the paper. I was afraid to look. "Suppose you tell me," I said.

Kathy licked her lips. "Somebody shot Mr. Royal last night. He's dead."

The bottom dropped out of my stomach. I went into my office and closed the door quietly behind me.

CHAPTER FIVE

It was all there, splashed across the front page in big type. There were pictures of John and Emmaline Royal and, on an inside page, a picture of the house on Peacock Hill and another showing a couple of white-jacketed attendants carting out the remains on a stretcher.

Royal, the story said, had been shot once through the heart. According to the grief-stricken widow, he had been reading in his den when she left the house around 8:45 to mail a letter. The mailbox was about fifty yards south of the driveway entrance. On the way back she had met Martha and Sam Proctor, her next-door neighbors who were taking their nightly constitutional. While exchanging pleasantries, they heard a shot.

It seemed to come from the Royal mansion and they rushed inside to find John Royal sprawled on the floor, dead. The book he had been reading lay open on the arm of his chair. The room showed no signs of struggle and, as far as the police could ascertain, nothing in the house had been disturbed. Because a wallet containing approximately two hundred dollars was found in the dead man's hip pocket, the police tentatively ruled out robbery as a motive.

Lieutenant Lew Gainey, who was in charge of the investigation, had checked all the doors and windows and found only one window open — in the den where Royal had died. Because of the air conditioning, everything else was closed tight, although a back door was unlocked. When she had recovered sufficiently to answer questions, Emmaline could not account for the open window. Lieutenant Gainey, in charge of the investigation, could not account for it either. It had not been used as a means of entrance or egress because the screen was locked from the inside.

The elderly couple, Mr. and Mrs. Proctor, corroborated Emmaline's story about the time of the shot. Sam Proctor was a retired businessman, and he and his wife were longtime residents of Arrowwood Road. Their reputation in Jellico was above reproach. Like Mrs. Royal, neither of them had seen or heard anything unusual prior to the shot.

It was evident that Lieutenant Gainey had precious little to go on. The bullet, a .32, had been examined by ballistics experts but the gun had not been located.

As for Riley Martin, he had been dining with a prominent businessman when the murder was committed. According to the host, Martin had left his apartment around ten o'clock. His alibi, Lieutenant Gainey conceded, was air-tight.

There was a lot of stuff about Royal and his vast business empire and, of course, about his many philanthropies. There was also a good deal about the Royal family history, how he was the last of the line, and how much his passing meant to the people of Hummock County in general and Jellico in particular. And then the final announcement that the Mosely Funeral Home was taking care of the interment, which would be in the Palms Cemetery.

And that was it.

As I pushed the paper aside, I felt a little better. At least Emmaline hadn't had anything to do with her husband's death.

But other things did bother me. Suppose Gainey found out that Emmaline and I had been seeing each other. I didn't know the lieutenant personally, but I'd heard that, besides being a very personable young man, he was a thorough workman with a nose for ferreting out the truth. The more I thought about it, the more uneasy I became. The police would check everyone connected with the Royals — and somewhere in their investigation they were going to find me. If Riley Martin had learned about Emmaline and me, it was a cinch the police would, too.

Also, there was the little matter of an alibi. I had none. At the moment Royal was shot, I was sitting in the woods waiting for his wife. I could see the skepticism on Gainey's face when I told him where I was — and why. And then something else hit me — if Emmaline told him that she'd had a date with me last night, it would cook her goose as well as mine. Especially when I had no alibi.

It was a hell of a situation.

About all I could do was sit tight and hope that Gainey wouldn't find out about us. But that was a long shot I knew wouldn't pay off. I could almost smell the polish on Gainey's badge.

I thought about calling Emmaline, in hope that we could line up some kind of story, but I figured the house on Arrowwood Road was still crawling with cops, so I let the idea go. I couldn't help wondering why she hadn't shown last night.

Julie called around ten, to tell me she'd read the story about Royal's murder.

"Isn't it awful, Neil?" she said. "Who do you think did it?"

"I haven't the slightest idea, honey," I said. "I didn't know him well enough. Somebody sure hated him, though."

"I suppose." She paused a few moments. "I don't suppose there's much chance of that housing project going through now, eh?"

"I'm afraid not, although Mrs. Royal could go through with it. You never know."

"Can we still build in Highland Shores, Neil?"

"Of course. It'll be a little tighter going, but we'll make it."

We blew kisses to each other over the phone and hung up. For the present, I figured, it would be best if I went about my business as if nothing had happened.

Business was slack and I had little to do but mope around the office. A couple of prospective house-buyers came in and I showed them what I had, but you sort of get a sixth sense about prospects in this business, and I knew they weren't really interested in buying. Just window-shopping. While I was downtown, I ordered a spray of gladioluses sent to the Mosely Funeral Home.

On the way home that night I bought a book of house plans. Julie and I studied it from cover to cover before deciding on one that had three bedrooms. It was laid out with a breezeway we wanted, facing the Gulf. We decided on a double garage against the day when I could afford a second car for Julie. Linda would be going to school in a year or so, and she'd need one.

The coroner's inquest was scheduled for Wednesday, the day before the funeral. It was being held in an anteroom of the Hummock County Courthouse, and at the last minute I decided to go. I had never attended an inquest before, and besides, I had a personal interest in this one.

The room was almost filled when I got there a few minutes before ten. As I said, John Royal was a big man, and big men, alive or dead, attract crowds. I found a seat in the rear of the oblong room. The only air conditioning consisted of a couple of lethargic ceiling fans, and I found myself shedding my coat and loosening my tie. The jury was already seated, and there was an air of expectancy in the room.

Emmaline and her brother arrived a few minutes after I did and were taken to a special section reserved for witnesses. She looked beautiful in black. There was a stir in the room as she walked to her seat, but she looked straight ahead, proud and defiant. Her brother looked as suave and urbane as usual, and I envied him his complacency.

Coroner Amos Phillips, a fussy little man with popping eyes, came in and sat behind a large table. After he got some papers straightened out in front of him, he explained that an inquest wasn't a trial and that there would be no cross-examination of witnesses.

"All we do here is try to ascertain the facts surrounding the violent death of John Cameron Royal," he said in a high voice. "We do not establish anyone's guilt. What we learn here today will be turned over to the grand jury for consideration. Keep that in mind."

A dapper, bespectacled young man, whom I recognized as Assistant State's Attorney Wilbur Hooks, rose to his feet and called Doctor Arthur Garrett to the stand. After being sworn in, Garrett testified that, as the county medical examiner, he had performed an autopsy on the body of John Royal and found that he had died as the result of a .32 caliber bullet penetrating his heart. Death, he said, had been instantaneous.

"I gather from your statement, Doctor, that Mr. Royal could not, and did not, grapple with his killer," said Hooks.

"That is correct." Dr. Garrett nodded.

"I have three witnesses who claim that they heard the fatal shot," Hooks said. "It was fired at or about nine o'clock on Monday evening, August eighth. Do you concur with this as the approximate time of death?"

Dr. Garrett frowned and examined his fingernails before answering. "I'd say so — yes."

"Thank you, Doctor. That will be all."

Sam Proctor was called next. He was a short, prune-faced little man who walked with a slight arthritic limp. He told how he and his wife, Martha, were taking their usual walk before retiring when they met Mrs. Royal.

"What did you talk about?" asked Hooks.

"The weather, mostly."

"And then what happened?"

Proctor said, "We bade each other good night and started to part company. We had hardly turned our backs, however, when there was a shot."

"You heard it very clearly?"

"Yes, sir. I did."

"And it came from the Royal home?" asked the attorney.

"Yes, sir. At least it seemed to. Actually, I didn't know where it came from, but Mrs. Royal screamed and ran toward her house. Martha and I followed her as quickly as we could."

"Did she reach Mr. Royal's den before you?"

"No, sir, we reached it together. She tripped and fell going up the porch steps. That's when we caught up with her."

"Describe what you saw in the den."

The old man fidgeted nervously. "Mr. Royal was lying on the floor," he said. "There was a red stain in the center of his shirt. I'm no doctor, but I could tell he was deader'n a mackerel!"

A few people tittered.

"What happened then?" pursued Hooks.

"Well, Mrs. Royal screamed again and dropped on the floor by her husband's body," said Proctor. "I pushed Martha out of the room and went to the telephone and called the police. They came a few minutes later."

"Did you see or hear anything unusual prior to the shot?"

Proctor shook his head. "No, sir, I didn't."

"No strangers? A car?"

"No, sir. Mrs. Royal was the only person on the street besides Martha and me."

Martha Proctor was a stoop-shouldered, sharp-featured woman in her late sixties, but she walked to

the witness chair with a firm step. Her story
corroborated her husband's in every detail except one.

"Mrs. Royal had more than turned her back on us
when we heard the shot," she said stubbornly. "She
was at least a hundred feet away."

Hooks smiled. "Thank you, Mrs. Proctor," he said.
"But I don't think thirty or forty steps one way or
another have much bearing on the case."

"Maybe so. But I thought I'd keep the record
straight."

Mrs. Proctor was excused and Lieutenant Lew
Gainey was summoned to the stand. Gainey was in
his early thirties. He was slightly above average
height, and had a trim, well-muscled figure. His curly
brown hair was parted on the side. He looked
extremely capable.

Gainey gave his name, age and rank as a member
of the Jellico Police Department.

"Suppose you tell us, Lieutenant, exactly what
happened last Monday night," urged Hooks.

Gainey folded his hands in his lap. "The call came
into my office around nine-ten," he said. "Sergeants
Max Wagner and Harley Foster accompanied me to
the Royal home. When we got there we found Royal
lying on the floor of his den. He was dead. There were
no signs of a struggle in the room. I told Wagner and
Foster to check the doors and windows while I went
to the living room to talk to Mrs. Royal."

"You didn't call Doctor Garrett?"

"I'm sorry," Gainey said. "I called him and the crime
lab before I went to question Mrs. Royal."

"Could you question her?" asked Hooks.

"Not right away — she was too upset. However, I talked to the Proctors and they told me what happened. Later, Mrs. Royal told me substantially the same story."

"Did you find any clues?"

"Not a clue exactly," replied Gainey thoughtfully. "About the only thing unusual was the open window in the victim's den."

Hooks folded his arms across his chest and frowned. "Why was an open window so unusual, Lieutenant?" he asked. "It was a warm, humid night."

"People don't usually open a window in the house when they have an air conditioning unit working," replied the officer.

"I see. Anything else?"

"A back door leading to the kitchen was closed, but unlocked. My men checked the grounds but were unable to come up with anything. Not even a footprint."

"And no murder weapon?"

"No, sir."

Hooks turned his back on Gainey and facing the jury, asked, "Then, as of this moment, you have no idea who killed John Royal?"

"That is correct, sir."

"One final question, Lieutenant," said Hooks. "I understand there are servants in the Royal household. Where were they when the murder was committed?"

"The Royals have an elderly couple named Anderson who take care of their needs around the place, and a maid," said Gainey. "The Andersons were asleep in their apartment over the garage and did not hear the shot. They weren't aware of anything until I awakened them. The maid sleeps out."

The lieutenant was excused and Emmaline Royal was called to the stand. Again there was a ripple of suppressed excitement as she walked to the chair. She was completely composed as she crossed her slim legs under the chair and faced Hooks.

Wilbur Hooks was nobody's fool. He handled her with kid gloves, and no wonder. As John Royal's widow and heir, she wielded a lot of power in the town, and he was quite aware of it. For several minutes he guided her gently over the territory already covered by the Proctors.

"Did Mr. Royal own a gun?" he asked.

"He owned a number of rifles," Emmaline said. "But if you're referring to a handgun, he did not. He wouldn't have one in the house."

"Do you own a gun?"

"No. I've never fired a weapon of any kind in my life."

Hooks removed his glasses, examined the lenses carefully, and then put them back on. "How long have you been married to John Royal?" he asked.

"We were married in June of last year."

"Since that time have you learned of anyone who disliked your husband enough to kill him?"

"No, I have not."

"Did Mr. Royal expect any visitors on the night he was murdered?" asked the attorney.

I could feel myself stiffen. He would have expected me — if Emmaline hadn't talked me out of it.

"Not that I know of," she said. "John was sitting in

his den, reading, so I presume he wasn't expecting anybody."

Hooks pursed his lips in thought. "Had Mr. Royal received any threatening letters or telephone calls?"

"If he had, he never told me."

And that was it. Hooks excused her at this point and, after a brief conference, the jury announced that John Cameron Royal had died at the hands of a person or persons unknown.

Everyone rose and began threading his way out of the room. A bevy of newspapermen and photographers followed Emmaline and her brother, asking questions and snapping pictures as they went. There was a tired smile on Emmaline's face as she talked to the reporters. She blinked once or twice when strobes popped around her, but all in all I thought she handled herself very well. As for Riley Martin, he was getting a kick out of the publicity. Maybe out of the murder as well, I thought. His sister stood to inherit half of Fort Knox.

I followed Emmaline and her brother at a distance as they walked down the courthouse steps to the white Chrysler. People stood around and gazed at her curiously. The crowd seemed strangely silent, as if weighing her. There was no jostling, no neck-craning or smart remarks. I paused on the top step to light a cigarette and decided to stay there, because it was a good vantage point from which to watch the Chrysler as it drove off.

Before getting into the car, Emmaline spotted me. Her eyes met mine and held. Riley Martin had already entered the car and, annoyed by her delay, followed her gaze. When he saw me, he angrily pulled her into the car and slammed the door. In a moment the Chrysler turned the corner and was out of sight.

So she had wondered if I'd show up. Now she knew.

The inquest had been interesting, but it hadn't answered my puzzles. Who was the man with the Spanish accent? And why hadn't Emmaline mentioned him on the stand? He was a nebulous figure, true, but the police have a habit of making nebulous figures come to life.

As I walked toward my car, I got the feeling that someone was watching me. Despite the midday heat, a cold, prickly sensation went up my spine. I was about to open the car door when I suddenly spun around and saw a fat little man with a bald head staring at me.

The moment our eyes met, he turned and strode hurriedly away.

CHAPTER SIX

The funeral was on Thursday, and Jellico observed a day of mourning for its leading citizen. Mayor Joe Maxey declared a holiday for the city employees and closed down City Hall. Some stores and many of the business firms shut down for a part of the day.

Only the banks, the post office and the more mercenary-minded inhabitants — like myself — stayed open. Flags were at half-staff, and many stores and private homes had wreaths on their front doors.

Despite the somber, heat-laden atmosphere, I received several telephone calls, one of which sent me over to Pine Needle Road to see a woman who wanted to sell her four-room bungalow. It was a nice home, neat and comfortable, but she wanted far too much for it. I agreed to list it, provided she came down a couple thousand. After a little haggling, she gave in.

It was nearly eleven o'clock when I headed back to the office. The silent, almost empty streets made me think of John Cameron Royal. Here was a man who really had everything, including a beautiful wife and a couple of million bucks, and yet an insignificant piece of lead, costing approximately eight cents, had reduced him to nothing. There was a moral there somewhere if I could only find it. Then I thought of Emmaline, and suddenly the day seemed brighter.

When I reached Longview Avenue, I changed my mind and turned left instead of right and headed for the cemetery. They'd be there now. Maybe I wanted to pay my respects to a man who deserved a better hand than life had dealt him. Maybe I was only making excuse to see Emmaline again, even if only from a distance.

The cemetery was crowded when I drove through the high wrought-iron gates, and a motorcycle cop wearing white cotton gloves frantically wig-wagged me to a parking spot some distance from the burial site. I lit a cigarette and walked back, threading my way among the tombstones. There was a green canopy over the spot where they were going to put John Royal, and several hundred people were gathered around it. I found myself on a slight elevation, which gave me a good view of the ceremony. After much eye-squinting, I located Emmaline. She was seated in the front row with Riley Martin and looked lovelier than ever in mourning.

The preacher was making his final eulogies in a voice so soft that I could not hear him from where I stood. The ceremony was reserved, impressive. But I couldn't help wondering if a hell-for-leather character like John Royal wasn't casting a cynical eye on the proceedings from some ethereal vantage point. Despite the solemn occasion, the thought brought a smile to my lips.

But it soon washed off when I saw Lieutenant Gainey. He was standing off to my left, about a hundred feet from the canopy. I could see his restless eyes studying each face as they raked over the silent crowd. The old saw about a killer attending the rites of his victim had probably brought Gainey to the cemetery. Despite the heat, a tiny icicle ran up and down my back. I knew that sooner or later the lieutenant and I were going to lock horns, and the prospect was not pleasant.

I was about to leave and avoid the heavy homeward traffic when I saw the other woman. She was standing slightly to the left of the preacher and, though she was strikingly good looking, I doubt I would have given her more than a passing glance if it hadn't been for the undiluted hate in her eyes as she stared at Emmaline and her brother, whose heads were bowed. If they were aware of the woman's presence, they gave no sign.

She intrigued me, and I moved to one side to get a better look at her. She was tall, slender, with coal-black hair cut in bangs above a delicately boned face. She appeared to be in her late twenties or early thirties. I followed her gaze again and there could be no mistake. Her eyes were focused venomously on the widow and her brother.

I wondered whether Gainey had noticed her too, and looked in his direction. But he was no longer where I had last seen him. I had to run my eyes over the assemblage several times before I finally found him. He had moved to a spot directly behind Emmaline and her brother, and he was looking at me!

I decided not to move or show any indication that I knew he was looking at me. I also decided not to look his way again, for fear of arousing his suspicions. He would get to me soon enough, and the longer I could postpone it the better. There was a chance that I was only another face in the crowd to him, and I returned my gaze to the black-haired woman. She was still there, her gaze riveted on Emmaline and her brother.

I wondered who she could be, and why she hated them so. Since Royal had left no blood relatives, she had to be someone out of their past, I reasoned. I was still studying her when she suddenly turned and looked at me. Our eyes held for several long moments before she looked away. Why had she singled me out of that crowd? Had she felt my eyes on her? Without the slightest idea why, I couldn't help wondering if she had seen me before.

I finally turned back to my car, my mind a maze of jumbled thoughts. I got in and smoked a cigarette before starting the engine and driving back to my office. Kathy was reading a movie magazine when I walked in.

She looked up. "Mrs. Royal called," she said, dropping her gaze back to the book. "She wants you to call her around five o'clock."

"What time did she call?"

"A few minutes after you left for Pine Needle Road."

I went into my office and tossed my Panama onto the leather couch. She must have called around nine-thirty, or just before she left for the church. I went to the window and stared at the row of backyards on the opposite street. It was Thursday and the washlines were empty. Well, I wouldn't call her. Not now or any time. What we had had was as cold as John Royal's body. Even so, my heart skipped a beat just thinking about her.

An elderly couple, Mr. and Mrs. Harvey Raulerson, 51 came in around two o'clock. They had just arrived from Toledo, Ohio, and were looking for a small bungalow in the $5,000 class. Florida has a Homestead Exemption Law, which provides that the first $5,000 of property valuation is tax-free, except for a small city tax. A lot of folks want that kind of property because it enables them to live within a small budget.

While we were talking, I thought of the woman over on Pine Needle Road and decided to call her. We had settled on a price of $5,500 for her house, but I figured she might come down $500 for a quick sale. I called her and she was agreeable.

We drove out to Pine Needle Road, and the Raulersons looked the house over. They liked it, and we sat down and talked business. In twenty minutes the whole thing was settled and I had a $500 deposit check in my pocket. I had only listed the house that morning, and in less than six hours it was sold. It happens that way sometimes.

I took the Raulersons back to their car, parked outside my office. They said they were going to Miami to visit their married daughter, but would be back in a week to close the deal and get the abstract and deed.

At four I let Kathy go for the day, hung around for a half hour and was about to close shop when the phone rang. It was my old lawyer friend, Bob Jamieson, who had sold me the Highland Shores property.

"You in some kind of trouble, Neil?" he asked.

"Not that I know of. Why?"

"It may not mean anything, but the missus and I were having lunch at the Patio Club this afternoon when we heard Harley Foster pumping one of the waiters about you."

My pulse rate jumped several notches. Harley Foster

was one of Lieutenant Gainey's boys. "Could you hear what it was about?"

"I heard enough to get a good idea," said Jamieson. "It sounded like Foster was trying to find out if you and Mrs. Royal had been in there lately." When I didn't answer, he went on: "I don't want to upset you, Neil, but Foster sounded like he meant business."

"Thanks, Bob," I said with more assurance than I felt. "They're probably making a routine check — a beautiful widow is always suspect, I guess. But all my deals were with John Royal. Foster's barking up the wrong tree."

"I hope so, I hear the food up in Raiford is terrible."

Raiford is the state penitentiary. "I've just lost my appetite," I said, laughing. "Thanks for calling."

I wasn't laughing, though, when I hung up. Gainey had already picked up my trail and was sicking his bloodhounds on me. Despite the fan, I was sweating and my hands were clammy. Gainey would ask questions, a lot of them, and unless I came up with the right answers, Raiford wasn't too remote a possibility.

Julie was watering the azaleas when I got home.

"Dinner's almost ready," she said, waving to me. "I'll be through in a few minutes."

I stopped in the middle of the living room and looked around at the clean, inexpensive furniture. I could hear Linda's squeals as she played with the Peterson kids next door. This house, small as it was, had sheltered us since before Linda was born. Every wall and floorboard contained some of our weakness and some of our strength. There was love here, understanding and tolerance. The intangibles of home were so strong I could almost reach out and touch them.

"Something wrong, dear?"

I started. I hadn't heard Julie come in. She was standing at my side, smiling up at me with impish eyes.

I grabbed her around the waist and whirled her round and round while she pumped her legs and squealed.

When I finally put her down, she gasped, "If you're so strong, Neil Cowan, you can mow the lawn right after dinner!"

While we were eating I told her about my trip to the cemetery, and she wanted to hear all the details.

"Mrs. Peterson was there too," she said when I finished. "She said it was very beautiful. And guess what. Lieutenant Gainey was there!"

"I saw him," I said, stirring my coffee. Linda cried in anguish when she dropped her spoon, and I had to get her another one.

"Do you think he was looking for the killer?" asked Julie.

"I wouldn't be surprised. He could have been there."

Julie's fork stopped halfway to her mouth. "He?" she said, frowning. "What makes you think a man killed Mr. Royal?"

"Just a figure of speech," I said. Julie's an avid who-done-it fan, and she likes to play detective while we're looking at TV.

"It could have been a woman," she went on thoughtfully. "Although I don't see why. He didn't play around, did he?"

I felt suddenly warm and got up and turned on the fan. "I wouldn't know," I said, hoping she would change the subject.

"If Mr. Royal was playing around, then he got what he deserved," she said firmly.

"You don't mean that."

A defiant look leaped into her eyes. "Why don't I?"

"Because you don't," I said, grinning. "You want a for-instance?"

"Yes, give me a for-instance."

"Okay. Suppose instead of being Mr. and Mrs. Neil Cowan that we were Mr. and Mrs. John Royal, and that somebody shot me. What would you say then? Would you be glad I was dead if you found out later I'd been playing around?"

It was twisting things around a bit, but there was enough similarity to draw a conclusion. I had to get a preview of how she'd feel if and when the roof fell in, especially since I had little doubt about the if, only the when.

"Oh, that's silly!" she exclaimed, getting to her feet and assembling the dishes on the tray. "You can't imagine anything as serious as that."

"Why not?"

"Because you can't! When two people love each other things like that don't happen."

I got up and wiped Linda's face with a napkin before she went out to play. "You're not only being naive, but you're evading the question," I said.

She put her arms on her hips and said, "Okay, you want an answer, so here it is. If something like that really happened to us, I'd still love you."

"Even if I'd been playing around with a nice, luscious redhead?"

She came around the table, put her arms around my neck and kissed me. "Even then," she said softly. "A woman can say she's going to do all kinds of things when she hears that her husband has been unfaithful, but if he's been good to her and she really loves him, she's only kidding herself. There's one real love during a lifetime, and nothing can destroy it. Nothing!"

Okay, so now I knew. She'd forgive me when the dam broke, and she'd still love me, too. It was nice to know, but somehow it didn't make me feel a damn bit better.

After drying the dishes, I changed to shorts and sneakers and went out and mowed the lawn. In a few minutes I was perspiring freely. The Petersons and their two kids drove off while I was working and waved at me. I grinned and waved back. They were rabid shuffleboard enthusiasts and often spent their evenings at the civic center, playing.

I finished the lawn and was almost through edging the walk when I happened to look up and see a car coming down the street. It was a 1952 two-door Chevy, dark blue, traveling slowly, and the driver was craning his neck as though looking for someone. He was. Me.

It was the little fat man I'd seen at the inquest.

CHAPTER SEVEN

My insides were churning as I watched the Chevy disappear down the street. I hadn't been wrong, the fat man had been looking for me. The expression on his face when he saw me was proof enough. But why was he interested in me? I didn't know him from Adam.

Then it hit me that he might be my mysterious caller on the day John Royal died. The thought excited me. If he was, he could have had something to do with the murder. The more I examined the idea, the more convinced I became that he was one person who might get me off the hook with Lieutenant Gainey. I could have kicked myself for failing to get his license number.

I finished the edging, laid the clippers aside and lit a cigarette. I had a feeling the fat man was no resident of Jellico. There were a lot of hotels, motels and rooming houses inside the city and out and tracking him down would be a full-time job. Since there was also a strong possibility that he lived in a nearby town, I decided to bide my time. Maybe the next time we met I would be in a better position to find out who he was.

There was a musical playing at the State Theatre that evening and Julie had a baby-sitter keep en eye on Linda while we took it in. Julie is nuts about musical pictures. It was after eleven when we got out and stopped at a diner for a snack before going home.

Some time during the night I saw the fat man again, but this time it was in a dream. I was lying in the middle of a dirt road, unable to move. I don't know what was the matter with me. I raised my head and saw him coming toward me in that blue Chevy. With each second its speed increased until it sounded like a herd of buffalo in full stampede. Then, at the very last instant, he twisted the wheel and the car missed me by inches. At that point I awoke, my body drenched with sweat.

Kathy had the mail opened and sorted when I got to the office the next morning. She looked glum, and I guessed she had had another spat with her boy friend, Willie Cahill.

"Willie again?" I said, glancing through the mail.

"Yeah," she said, flushing. "He stood me up again last night." When I did not say anything, she asked, "What can a girl do with a knucklehead like that, Mr. Cowan?"

"Does he stand you up often?"

"Every week or so."

"How about excuses?" I asked.

"Oh, he's got some lulus," she said, pouting. "But they're as phony as a movie scene."

I smiled. "Why don't you stand him up for a change?" I suggested. "The trouble is, Willie's too sure of you."

The idea pleased her, and her face was beaming when she went back to her desk. Beatrice Fairfax Cowan, that's me. I was a fine one to give advice to the lovelorn when I was sitting atop a marital bomb myself.

At ten o'clock I drove over to Bob Jamieson's to get the abstract on the Highland Shores lot and pay him for the balance. He was in court, but his secretary had the papers ready for me. I gave her my check and left. I was crossing the lobby when someone tugged at my sleeve and I turned. It was Emmaline.

She looked like a blonde goddess in a black satin dress with a narrow white collar. Her eyes were softly compliant, and I could feel my insides jump.

"How are you, Neil?" she asked quietly.

"I'm fine," I said. "Sorry about — your husband."

"It's been a nightmare," she said in a tired voice.

"It's always a trying time." I tried to feel sorry for her, but couldn't. Directly involved or not, she had wanted John Royal dead.

"Thanks for the flowers. They were lovely."

I nodded. People flowed by us, and we moved closer to the wall, out of their way.

"Can't we go somewhere and talk?"

"I'm afraid not," I said. Then, because it was on my mind, I asked, "Why didn't you show up that night?"

"What night?"

So that's how it's going to be, I thought bitterly. "You were supposed to meet me last Monday night, remember?"

"Oh, yes! Now I remember." She shook her head in disgust. "Please forgive me, Neil. Something came up at the last minute and I couldn't make it."

"You couldn't have phoned to let me know?"

"It was too late. You had already left the office, and I couldn't call your home, could I?"

"No, you couldn't," I admitted, "But it leaves me out

in left field. I have the motive — or Gainey will think so — and no alibi for the time your husband was murdered."

It took her several moments to catch on. "You mean the police?" Then she laughed. "Don't be silly, darling! They couldn't possibly think you had anything to do with John's murder."

I wished I were as certain of it as she was. "Then it'll be okay if I tell them we were supposed to meet that night?" I asked.

Emmaline paled. "Neil, you can't!" she said anxiously. "You know how they will jump to conclusions!"

Of course I knew, and I was sorry I had suggested it "I won't say anything," I promised. "But I'll have to come up with something that will stand up, or I'll be in a tight spot."

Emmaline was trying to convince me that my fears were groundless when my attention was drawn to a man lounging near the cigar stand. He was watching us. He was tall and athletic-looking.

"Don't turn around right away," I said, interrupting her. "There's a man standing near the cigar stand watching us. After a while sneak a look and tell me — have you ever seen him before?"

Emmaline opened her handbag, took out a compact and pretended to fix her face. She studied the man for several moments in the mirror before returning it to her handbag.

"I know him," she said in a tight voice. "His name is Max Wagner. He's one of the detectives who came to the house the night John was murdered."

Which meant that Gainey was having one or both

of us followed. I grimaced. We were certainly making things easy for him, meeting like this.

"We'd better break this up," I said. "Gainey will get ideas when he gets Wagner's report."

Emmaline agreed. We shook hands and I went outside to my car. As I pulled out of the parking lot, I glanced in the rear-view mirror to see whether Wagner was tailing me. He wasn't.

Kathy had a scared look on her face when I walked into the office a few minutes later. "You've got company," she said.

He was looking out the window, smoking a cigarette. It was Lieutenant Gainey. When he saw me he turned and smiled.

"Your secretary said it would be all right for me to wait," he said. His voice was low, courteous, at the same time noncommittal. He opened a wallet and showed me a badge. "I'm Lieutenant Lew Gainey."

I closed the door, scaled my hat onto the couch and nodded. "I know. I saw you at the inquest." When he didn't say anything, I asked, "What can I do for you, Lieutenant?"

He selected one of the leather armchairs, pulled an ashstand close and crossed his legs. "Let's dispense with the sparring, shall we?" he said quietly. His face remained pleasant enough, but his eyes were unfriendly. "You know why I'm here."

"Fair enough," I said. I lit a cigarette and exhaled deeply. "You're here because you've heard that I was in several drinking spots with Mrs. Royal. Being a cop, you figure that where there is smoke, there usually is fire. Well, you're quite right. There was lots of fire."

If I thought that my direct approach would bowl him over, I was disappointed. His expression didn't change.

"Thank you," he said. "I admire your frankness, Mr. Cowan. You had an affair with Mrs. Royal then?"

"I guess you could call it that, yes."

"What else would you call it?"

I smiled. "There are several names for it," I said. "Such as having a fling or sowing one's wild oats. There are many others." My complacency surprised me. I paused and said, "But please remember, Lieutenant, I didn't have to break her arm."

"I'm sure you didn't." He made a steeple of his hands. "How did you meet Mrs. Royal?"

I told him about my Lake Chicopee deal with her husband.

"I understand you had some trouble with the family," he said.

"Trouble?"

"Yes. Didn't Mr. Martin threaten you if you didn't stop seeing his sister?"

Good old Riley. "He threatened me, yes," I nodded. "But I didn't take him seriously."

"Why not? He looks like he could take you."

I grinned. "He probably could, but it still didn't worry me."

Gainey studied me for several moments in silence. "Nothing worries you, does it, Mr. Cowan?" When I shrugged in answer, he asked, "Does your wife know about your nocturnal activities?"

I winced. He had hit a soft spot. "No."

"I understand you have a little girl of five?"

"Yes."

"Were you in love with Mrs. Royal?" he snapped suddenly.

It was a loaded question, but I decided to tell him the truth. "I thought I was," I said.

"And you're not now?"

"No."

"When did you realize you weren't in love with her, before or after Mr. Royal was shot?" asked Gainey.

"Before."

He seemed surprised. "Oh? What made you change your mind?"

Because she had asked me to kill him, you stupid jerk! "Nothing in particular," I said. "I just figured I was making a fool of myself."

"I see." I could tell by his eyes he didn't believe me. He squashed out his cigarette and leaned forward, like a panther ready to spring. "Now we come to the night of the murder," he said. "Where you were around nine o'clock?"

I'd been giving this question a lot of thought all week, and I was as ready for it as I'd ever be. "Let's see. I left the house around eight-ten that night," I said. "I drove over to Highland Shores to inspect a lot my wife and I had just bought. I stayed about fifteen minutes and left."

"Did you get out of the car?"

"No."

"All right. Go on."

"I drove to Michael Swain's house. He's also in the real estate business, and we often collaborate on selling a piece of property. That is, we both list it and split the commission."

"What time did you get there?" asked Gainey.

"About ten minutes of nine, give or take a few minutes. He wasn't home, so I waited outside in the car. I figured he and Janice were out shopping and would return shortly. They seldom go anywhere at night."

"But he didn't show up?" His eyes were hooded pools of skepticism.

"No, he didn't. I waited until ten o'clock and then I drove downtown and went into the drug store to make a telephone call. I was going to call a friend of Mike's to ask him where he was but I finally decided not to. I went back to my car and drove home."

"Didn't you have an encounter with Mr. Martin on the way?"

"Yes, I'm sorry. We only talked a few minutes."

"Was his attitude still antagonistic?" he asked.

"Yes, but in a jocular sort of way."

Gainey frowned. "Did you get in touch with Mr. Swain the next day?"

"No. I found out that he'd left town the previous afternoon for a week's vacation. His wife went with him."

Gainey lit another cigarette, studied the glowing end and shook his head. "You've got no alibi," he said. "You know that, don't you, Mr. Cowan?"

"Yes, I realize it," I said. "Why should I? I had no reason to think I'd need to account for my movements that night. Take my word for it, Lieutenant. I did not kill Mr. Royal."

"Do you own a gun?"

"No."

"But you know how to use one?"

"Yes. I was in the army for two years."

"How many times were you on Peacock Hill?"

"Three," I said thoughtfully. "Once when Mr. Royal sent for me, a second time when he gave me a deposit on the Lake Chicopee property, and the third time when I gave him the deed and the abstract to the land."

Gainey nodded. "Do you have any theories about who killed him?"

I hesitated. Should I tell him about the guy with the Spanish accent? It might not mean anything, but telling it could possibly put me in good standing as a cooperative suspect.

I told him about the telephone call I'd received on the morning of the murder. But instead of telling him that Emmaline had talked me out of keeping the appointment, I explained that I had turned it down because of my intention to see Mike Swain. I don't know why, but I didn't say anything about the little fat man.

Gainey asked a lot of questions about the telephone call, and one of them was whether I thought that my anonymous caller had disguised his voice. It was an angle I hadn't thought of, but I told him I didn't think so. He finally ran out of questions and got up to go.

"Okay, Mr. Cowan, that'll be all for now," he said. "I hope you won't make any rash moves."

"Like what?"

"Like leaving town without letting us know where

you can be reached," he said.

I sat there for a long time after he left, smoking and thinking. I was on the spot, but good. Gainey would do a thorough job of trying to find Royal's killer, but if I were in his shoes, I'd consider a guy named Neil Cowan as my number one suspect. This Cowan guy not only had been playing around with the victim's wife, but he had no alibi for the time of the murder. Cowan had both motive and opportunity, the two most important knots in the hangman's noose.

Julie's and Linda's pictures were on my desk, and the sight of their smiling faces made me want to cry. I tried to blame Emmaline for my predicament, but I couldn't. She had been like any healthy young animal who craves sexual satisfaction. I happened to come along at exactly the right time. There was only one thing wrong — I hadn't been content to let it end that first time in the back seat of her car. I had had to make a production of it.

Kathy went out to lunch. While she was gone, I continued to mope around the office. I had a hunch that Gainey would devote his time from now on to trying to tie me in with the murder. Not that I blamed him. He was doing a job, and I stood out like a sore thumb. Which meant I could either sit back and wait for the axe to fall, or I could do something about John Royal's murder.

I decided to try to find the killer myself.

Summing everything up, I had three things to go on: one, the man who spoke with the Spanish accent; two, the little fat man in the dark-blue Chevy; and three, the open window in John Royal's den the night he was murdered. I was no detective, but I had a feeling that learning the answer to any one of them would bust the case wide open.

I was trying to figure out where I could start, when the phone rang. I scooped up the receiver. "Yes?" I said.

"Mr. Cowan?" It was a woman's voice, soft and cultured.

"That's right."

"My name is Lynn Barton." She paused, as if trying to make up her mind to go on. "You don't know me, but I'd appreciate it very much if you will come to my apartment tonight."

"Do you wish to buy or sell?" I inquired.

"Neither, Mr. Cowan. You see, I'm the woman you were looking at in the cemetery yesterday."

CHAPTER EIGHT

It was a few minutes after eight when I eased the Plymouth into a parking spot outside the Brighton Apartments. The building was less than five years old, a modernistic, six-story affair of pink stucco. It was U-shaped, and there were separate entrances for each wing. Lynn Barton lived in the west wing, apartment 2-B.

My mind was a conglomeration of conflicting thoughts as I stood outside her oak-paneled door and pressed the little white button. There was a hurried tap of high heels and the statuesque woman I had seen in the cemetery opened the door. She wore black velveteen lounging slacks, a white silk blouse and gold-tinted pumps.

She smiled and stepped aside, and I went into a large, air-conditioned room that was the ultimate in chrome-and-leather furnishings. The rug was ankle deep, the lighting indirect and the beige draperies had little vermilion-colored circles on them. The walls were bare except for a couple of excellent Mondrian reproductions that complemented the furnishings perfectly.

Lynn Barton was even more attractive close up. Her eyes were sea green, and her slim, high-waisted figure moved with an easy grace that suggested ballet training. She waved me to a leather chair and I made myself comfortable. She offered to fix me a drink but I shook my head.

She regarded me pensively for several moments and said, "I asked you to come here, Mr. Cowan, because I think we have something in common."

"Mrs. Royal and her brother?"

"Yes. Because they are of extreme interest to us both, I have a favor to ask you. I would appreciate it very much if you would hold an envelope for safekeeping."

I leaned back against the cushion. "How do you come to know about me?" I asked.

She crossed slim legs and smiled. "Despite its growing pains, Jellico is still a small town in many respects, Mr. Cowan," she said. "People like to talk, and there has been plenty of gossip about you and that woman on Peacock Hill."

What she said surprised and shocked me. I had no idea that Emmaline and I had become the topic of public interest and the first thought that came to my mind was a hope that Julie hadn't heard any of it. I didn't think she had, but a sudden uncertainty gnawed at me.

"It's too late to undo the past," I said, "but it happens to be finished."

"I guessed as much," said Lynn. "Otherwise I would not have called you. In fact, during the thirteen weeks I've been in Jellico, I have made it my business to learn all about you."

"Because of my affiliation with the Royals?"

"Yes. I also have a feeling that you are, at the moment, Lieutenant Gainey's number one suspect."

I took a pack of cigarettes from my pocket, shook a couple loose and gave her one. Then I lit them. Lynn Barton was pretty sharp, I thought, exhaling. I was beginning to wonder whether she also knew who had killed John Royal.

"Do you think I killed Mr. Royal?" I asked.

"I know you didn't," she said flatly.

"Your confidence is reassuring." I studied her for several moments. "Could it be because you killed him?"

Her laugh had a pleasant sound. "No, I did not kill him," she said with equal firmness. "I did not even know the man. It is my belief that either Mrs. Royal or her brother killed him."

I shook my head. "That's physically impossible," I said. "Mrs. Royal was at least a hundred feet from the house when the shot was fired. And she's got a couple of reliable witnesses to back her up. As for Riley Martin, he was with a local businessman from seven until nearly ten o'clock that night." I paused and then said, "Unless, of course, you think they hired someone to do it."

"They hired no one."

"And yet you're convinced that one of them shot Mr. Royal?"

"Yes."

"Have you figured out what sort of legerdemain was used?"

She squashed out her cigarette in a tray. "No, I haven't But believe me, Mr. Cowan, no magic was used."

"About this envelope," I said, changing the subject. "Does it have anything to do with their guilt?"

"Only indirectly." She stared at her gold slipper. "However, the information in it is very enlightening, and might open Lieutenant Gainey's eyes."

"How long am I to hold this envelope?"

"It depends entirely on the circumstances."

It hit me then why she wanted me to hold the envelope, and the realization stunned me. "You want me to take it to the police in case something should happen to you," I said. "Your life then, is in danger."

"You are an astute man, Mr. Cowan."

"Why don't you go to the police?" I asked.

She shook her head. "I can't," she said. Her voice was edged with frustration. "I don't have any proof."

"This letter won't clarify things?" I asked, interrupting her.

"It's a step in the right direction but, unfortunately, not nearly enough for conviction." She got to her feet and roamed restlessly around the room. "You have every right to refuse, Mr. Cowan. It could put you in extreme danger."

"From whom?"

She shrugged. "As I've just said, I have no proof that Mrs. Royal or her brother either killed or engineered the death of John Royal," she said. "And I could very well be mistaken about their guilt. All I'm going on is a woman's intuition." She looked at me and smiled. "That isn't very much to go on, is it, Mr. Cowan?"

I didn't know how to take this strange and beautiful woman. Somewhere in her past she had come across Emmaline and her brother, and from that contact had blossomed a hate so strong it had warped her judgment. I wondered what had happened and, clairvoyantly, she sensed what I was thinking.

"Please don't ask me, Mr. Cowan," she said, her eyes somber. "Later, perhaps, but not now."

"You don't trust me."

"That isn't true," she said. She weighed her next words carefully. "Let us say the time isn't appropriate for a complete confession."

"But you did know Mrs. Royal and her brother before they came to Jellico?" I probed.

"Yes."

"Quite intimately?"

"Yes," she said, hesitating. Her eyes pleaded with me.

"Please, Mr. Cowan."

"And you won't see Gainey?" I asked.

She shook her head impatiently. "With what? Suspicions, hunches, intuitions? He's going to want more than that. Much more."

She was right, of course. A good cop plays his hunches, sure, but they are his own hunches. He rarely has faith in someone else's.

I got up, reached for my hat and fumbled with it. There didn't seem to be anything else to say.

"I'll get the envelope," she said, disappearing into another room. She returned a few moments later with a long white envelope and handed it to me.

I put it in my pocket. "How do you know I won't give it to Lieutenant Gainey?" I asked.

She smiled. "Because I know you, Mr. Cowan. Despite the *affaire d'amour,* shall we say, I am convinced that you are an honorable man."

"Thank you," I said, putting a finger on my lips.

"I think I'll be safe as long as they think someone else has the envelope."

I tried to catch her off guard. "By 'they' I suppose

you mean Mrs. Royal and her brother?"

But she only smiled. "Perhaps."

She walked with me to the door. "I hold the envelope," I said. "Then what happens?"

She said earnestly, "You'll know what to do when the time comes."

I left shortly afterwards and went back to my car. The night was warm, humid, but I sat for several minutes, thinking. The temptation to open the envelope was strong, but I finally decided against it. Next, I tried to think of where to hide it. I couldn't hope to conceal it at home. Julie might find it and get curious, and Linda was always poking into something.

The office seemed the only logical place.

I drove there. I pulled the blinds before snapping on my desk lamp. I looked around. At first glance, no place seemed even reasonably secure. It would have to be a perfect spot because there was a chance that two lives, including mine, depended on its safekeeping. I spent more than an hour examining every nook and corner of the two rooms without finding anything that satisfied me. It wasn't until I went into the lavatory that I found what I was looking for.

The space between the toilet bowl tank and the wall was so close that I had never until now noticed it. I found a nine-by-twelve manila envelope, put the white envelope into it and, with some difficulty, pushed it behind the tank.

Nobody would dream of looking for it there — I hoped.

I switched out the lights, locked the door and went back to my car. I had just pulled out of the driveway when I glanced at the rear-view mirror and saw a car easing out from the curb behind me. Even in the uncertain light I could see it was the dark-blue Chevy.

This was the chance I'd been waiting for. If I could maneuver the little fat man into a corner, there was a chance I might find out a few things. I drove south on Longview, past neat rows of frame bungalows and turned right on Roof Street. The Chevy did the same, keeping approximately a block behind. This was a semi-residential neighborhood, and there was no place where I could maneuver him into leaving his car. I tried to think of a plan, but things were happening too fast. First, Lynn Barton and her mysterious envelope, and now my fat little friend. I wondered if he had followed me to her apartment, and got a funny feeling in the pit of my stomach.

I swung left on Riverhill Road. Here was an area of gas stations, cheap diners with gaudy neons, used car lots and an occasional factory. To my left was the new Amalgamated Carbon building. Thinking of factories reminded me of Jim Haviland's place and an idea came to me. Jim owned a small plastics firm on Rumar Road. It was a one-story building with a single front entrance next to a narrow alley. If I parked outside the building and slipped into the alley, maybe my shadow would think I'd gone into the building and leave his car long enough to investigate. It was worth a try.

Rumar Road was the next street and I turned right. The factory was only a few doors from the corner and, fortunately for my plan, there were no cars in front of the building. I drew up to the curb, switched off the engine and hurried into the alley. Pressing myself against the wall, I didn't have to wait long. The Chevy went by slowly, and I could see the little fat man looking the building over. The car disappeared out of my range down the street, but I still didn't move. If he was curious, he'd come snooping back.

I stood tense and expectant, listening for the hum of a car motor, a footstep, anything. But the street remained quiet. From somewhere I could hear the hoot of a train whistle. Even though the alley was cool and damp, I was perspiring freely. The minutes ticked by with no sign of my little fat friend. It was beginning to look as if my idea was a flop when I caught the sound of an approaching footstep.

The footsteps stopped in front of the building. He was so close I could hear his breathing. He was standing near the door he thought I'd entered. This was it. I stepped quickly from the alley. At the sound, he swung his head in my direction, a wild, frightened gleam in his eyes.

He turned to run, but he wasn't built for speed. My leaping tackle caught him around the waist. We fell to the ground, twisting and squirming in silent fury. He was incredibly strong, and knew every dirty trick in the trade. He swung for my throat with the side of his hand, missed and caught me on the jaw, stunning me. When the blow didn't loosen my hold, he brought up his knee, catching me sharply in the groin. Pain forced an exclamation past my lips, I swung at his jaw, my fist hitting the top of his head solidly.

We managed to get to our feet somehow, still struggling violently. Again he brought up his knee, but this time I anticipated the kick and arched my body backward just in time. We were breathing heavily now, but instead of growing weaker, he seemed to be getting stronger. And he was not bad at infighting. I couldn't get a good grip on him. Twice he almost wrenched free, but each time I caught him at the last moment and held on despite the punishing blows from his hands and knees.

There was a shout from somewhere and for a fraction of a second it distracted me. That was what he needed. He swung his heavy body toward me, propelling me backward against my car. My head hit the fender with such force that I was momentarily stunned. Before I could get my bearings, he was gone.

I was on my knees when somebody lifted me to my feet. It was a white-haired old man with a leathery face and the body of a Mack truck.

"What the devil's going on?" he asked, peering at me intently. "You hurt, mister?"

I tried a grin. "I'm okay." I felt the back of my head. It was tender to the touch, but the skin wasn't broken.

"Did he try to mug you?" he wanted to know. "There's been a lot of it going on around here lately."

I nodded, content to let it go at that. "He didn't get anything," I said.

"I live next door to the factory," he explained. "When I heard the scuffle, I came out to see what was up. I got a good look at him, mister."

I walked to my car and got in. The old man leaned in the open window and studied me for several moments.

"Sure you don't want me to call the cops?" he asked.

"No point in making a fuss — he was probably just after the price of another drink. No harm done."

He looked at me dubiously. "Well, if that's the way you want it, young man," he said.

"Thanks," I said, starting the car. "You came along just in time."

He nodded, pleased. "If I'd gotten here a few moments sooner, we'd have had him."

On the drive home I cursed myself for blowing an opportunity to corral the fat man. I was sure now that he was involved in some way with John Royal's murder. The fury with which he fought me indicated as much. Since he hadn't spoken during the brief struggle, I still had no way of knowing whether he was the man with the Spanish accent. I was so mad I slammed my palm against the steering wheel.

I was halfway home when I thought of Lynn Barton and the possibility that the fat man had followed me from her apartment building. Acting on impulse, I braked outside an all-night drug store on the corner of Kipling Street. I went in and asked information for her telephone number, dialed it.

"Yes?" her voice was low, cautious.

"This is Neil Cowan," I said. "Are you all right?"

"Yes. Shouldn't I be?"

"I just wanted to be sure." Then I told her about my encounter with the fat man.

"Why is he following you?" she asked when I was finished.

"I wish I knew." I described him in detail and asked if she knew him.

"No," she said thoughtfully. "And I doubt he has

anything to do with Mrs. Royal or her brother."

"What makes you say that?"

"I'm not sure. Call it intuition."

We talked for several minutes without getting anywhere. She promised to keep in touch and we hung up. By the time I left the booth my head was throbbing worse than ever and nausea was developing in the pit of my stomach. I sat at the counter and a blonde waitress sauntered over.

"Bromo," I said.

She gave me a knowing smile. "I know what you mean," she said. She shook her head. "Boy, did I tie one on last night!"

After I downed the bromo, I went into the washroom. I wanted to see what I looked like after my set-to with the fat man. As far as I could see, there wasn't a scratch on me, and my clothes looked okay.

Back in the car, I wondered about Lynn Barton. She was like some cloak-and-dagger character, with TV trimmings. Slightly unbelievable. But so was the rest of this mess — which had started with a simple real estate deal.

Maple Street was dark when I swung into it a few moments later. Maybe it was because my senses were becoming attuned to danger, maybe I was suddenly suspicious of everything and everyone. I don't know. But I spotted the dark-colored Dodge the moment I turned the corner. The man sitting behind the wheel slid down in the seat when my headlights crossed his car. Although I caught only a fleeting glimpse of his face, I recognized Detective Max Wagner, the man who had been watching Emmaline and me in the

Westminster Building that morning.

Lieutenant Gainey wasn't taking any chances of his pigeon leaving town.

Julie was having her bedtime snack when I got home. I was surprised to find that, despite all that had happened, it was only a few minutes after eleven.

"How did it go?" she asked, flashing me one of her wonderful smiles.

"Fine," I said. "Mr. Snyder wants me to sell his house for him."

There was no Mr. Snyder. It was just another of the many lies I'd been telling Julie lately.

I was sipping my coffee when Julie said, "You had a call tonight, Neil. Some man with a Spanish accent."

I put my coffee cup down carefully. "What did he want?"

"He didn't say. He just asked to speak to you, and when I told him you weren't home he thanked me and hung up."

My sins were coming home to roost, and I didn't like it. No matter what happened, I didn't want Julie or Linda involved.

"What time did he call?" I asked.

Julie screwed her face into a frown. "Let me see. 'M-Squad' was about half over, I think. About nine-fifteen."

I had to smile. Julie times everything with her television programs. We finished our coffee. Julie went upstairs and while I was putting out the lights the phone rang. The sound was unusually loud and shrill in the darkened house. I picked up the receiver.

"Hello."

There was no answer. The silence was almost

complete, but not quite. I could hear someone breathing slowly, heavily.

"Who's there?" I asked again.

This time there was a click. The line was dead. My caller had hung up.

CHAPTER NINE

The next day was Saturday, and I slept a little later than usual. My arms and legs ached and the back of my head was still throbbing. Breakfast was flat and tasteless and, to add to my gray mood, it started to rain while I was driving to the office. I kept glancing in the rear-view mirror, but if anyone was tailing me, I couldn't detect it.

Business was slow again. What with the rain, there wasn't much I could do but mope around the office. No calls came in and that surprised me, for I expected my Spanish friend to phone again. It was he who had refused to talk to me last night, I was sure. What he had hoped to gain by not saying anything was beyond me.

Around eleven I went into the washroom to check on the envelope. I played a pencil flashlight on the narrow aperture between the wall and the tank. Everything seemed as I had left it last night.

Kathy went out at noon. A few minutes later I heard a car come into the driveway. It was a new Ford Galaxie, and the guy behind the wheel in the transparent raincoat was Bob Jamieson.

Bob was tall, skinny and about my age, though his thinning hair and rounded shoulders make him look older. A nicer guy never lived, and he's one of the best lawyers in Hummock County.

He came in looking as gloomy as the day. "I've just come from the D.A.'s office, Neil. According to my good friend, Wilbur Hooks, you're in a bind."

"John Royal?"

Jamieson nodded. "Hooks had just finished talking to Gainey when I walked in," he said. "Gainey thinks you could be involved in the old man's murder. They apparently haven't enough for an indictment, but they're sure going to keep trying."

I exhaled deeply on my cigarette and said nothing. It was quiet in the room. The rain splattered against the windows monotonously. I felt cold and depressed.

"Care to tell me?" he asked.

There was a worried look in his deep-set eyes. I knew he was suffering with me. There are guys like that. He sat there making like a priest while I told him everything that had happened, from John Royal's telephone call to my encounter with the little fat man on Rumar Road last night. I omitted mention of Lynn Barton and her mysterious envelope. I wanted to keep one hole card.

"Does Gainey know all this?" he asked when I'd finished.

"Everything except about the little fat man."

"Why didn't you tell him about that?"

I shrugged. "I don't know. I guess it didn't seem important at the time."

Bob was quiet for several minutes, chewing on what I'd told him. Finally he squashed out his cigarette and said, "They don't have enough for an indictment now. But things could change."

"How?"

"I have a feeling that somebody's got you down for a patsy. Sure you've never owned a gun?"

"Of course."

"How about Julie?"

I shook my head. "She's scared to death of them. Why is the gun so important?"

Bob got up and went to the window. "If you are being set up as the killer, they'll have to tie the murder weapon to you. Be very careful, Neil. If Gainey should find the gun anywhere on your property — your office, car, house, even buried in your backyard — Hooks could get an indictment in ten minutes."

It was a frightening thought. Innocent people are being framed all the time and not only on television. You read about real-life miscarriages of justice often enough.

"Why would anyone want to frame me?" I asked, but the answer, of course, was obvious. He would want a fall-guy, and my affair with Emmaline made me the logical choice. It gave me the strongest possible motive.

Bob turned away from the window and studied me for several moments. "How long have we known each other, Neil?" he asked.

I grinned. "Hell, we grew up together and went through school together. Why do you ask?"

"I want you to tell me the truth. Did you kill John Royal?"

My eyes held his. "As God is my judge, Bob, I did not," I said.

Bob slipped into his raincoat. "Okay, here is what you do, if Gainey should pick you up for questioning — cooperate with him a hundred per cent, as you have. But the moment he starts getting rough, tell him you're not saying another word until you send for me.

Got it?"

I got to my feet to walk him to the door. "Thanks, Bob," I said.

He slapped my arm playfully and left. It was still raining as I watched him back out of the driveway and head north on Longview.

Linda wanted to go to Woodbridge Park on Sunday, and since Julie had already made plans to wash and set her hair, she coaxed me into taking her.

Woodbridge Park is one of Jellico's proudest possessions. It was named after Colonel Jeffrey Solomon Woodbridge, one of Lee's most able officers during the Civil War. Unlike old Jonathan Royal, who had come to Jellico after the war, the colonel had practically founded the town. At his death in 1888, he had willed the town the family estate. Although his intention had been that the land be used to perpetuate his name, the town fathers did nothing until shortly after World War I, when a historically minded commissioner got the bright idea to turn the estate into a park. A man-made lake was added, along with a horse-back statue of the colonel brandishing his sword.

At the entrance to the park I bought Linda a bag of peanuts to feed to the squirrels. The morning was beautiful, sun-drenched, and the section reserved for the septuagenarian checker-players was crowded. We walked past the old colonel's statue and found an empty bench under a huge red mulberry tree.

"Daddy, there's squirrel!" exclaimed Linda, clapping her hands excitedly and pointing. She looked cute in a white faille dress with a narrow blue ribbon. I quickly unshelled a couple of peanuts and gave them to her. In a moment she was scurrying off with another girl her own age.

Reality was quiet and peaceful in the shade of the big tree, and I found it hard to believe that, figuratively, I was up to my neck in quicksand. Linda came back for a second helping of peanuts and was off again. I was wondering what tomorrow would bring when someone sat down on the bench next to me. Even before I turned, I knew it was Emmaline.

She was disturbingly lovely in a pleated white linen dress with black dots, elbow-length gloves and black kid pumps. Even through my awareness that she was pure danger to me, I couldn't help responding to her womanhood.

"How did you know I was here?" I asked.

She smiled. "You don't mind my finding you, do you?"

"No — I don't mind." In a perverse way, I didn't.

She studied me. "Are you still angry at me?"

I turned and faced her. "Dammit, what good can come of our seeing each other like this? Suppose Wagner or another one of Gainey's stooges tailed you here? You know Gainey's baying on my trail. If he nails me, you'll be smeared, too. I should think you'd want to be careful — for your own sake."

"Did you kill John?"

I was so surprised my mouth popped open. "Are you serious?"

She placed a gloved hand over mine. "Forgive me, Neil," she said contritely. She looked down at her well-shod feet, and for a moment I thought she was going to cry. "I know you won't believe me, but you're the only man I've really and truly cared for."

"No, I don't believe it," I said harshly. "A woman doesn't ask the man she loves to kill for her."

"That was a mistake. I've been sorry ever since. It was just that — I wanted you so. I was nearly insane — "

There was a tug at my sleeve. It was Linda, and she was looking at Emmaline with dark, inquisitive eyes.

"What's the lady's name, Daddy?" she asked, holding her hand out for more peanuts.

I couldn't tell Linda the truth. She had a genius for remembering names, and Emmaline Royal might cause some eyebrow-lifting in the little house on Maple Street.

"This is Mrs. Isabel Snyder, dear," I said. "Her husband is a client of mine."

Emmaline reacted admirably. "So this is Linda!" she exclaimed, taking one of Linda's pudgy hands. "My, what a pretty young lady!"

Linda withdrew her hand and curtsied so smartly that I had to laugh.

"Thank you, ma'am," she said. "Now excuse me, I have to go feed the squirrels."

There was a wistful look in Emmaline's eyes as she watched her go. "She's a darling, Neil," she said.

"Thanks."

Neither of us spoke for several minutes, the silence hanging heavy between us. Emmaline watched Linda trying to entice a squirrel with a peanut. As for me, I took the opportunity to study her. This was, I hoped, our last meeting — but I couldn't help hoping that things might have gone differently for us. Once I had been willing to face losing Julie and Linda to possess her. She had changed that with a word, putting our affair in its proper, sordid perspective. But she still drew me physically like a powerful magnet.

"Neil?"

I looked away guiltily. "Yes?"

"It's all over between us, isn't it?"

I hesitated so long in answering that she put a hand on my arm. I looked at her and couldn't answer. The words were there — words to accept her, to deny her — there seemed to be two of me, both trying to talk at the same time, and both unwilling to make a commitment. They got as far as my lips and no farther.

Our eyes were still probing each other when we heard the footsteps and a shadow on the walk materialized into a man.

It was Riley Martin.

I looked at him, at his face flushed with anger, his eyes pinpoints of hate. Suddenly I felt a deep loathing for the whole rotten mess, for myself and for Emmaline and for the man who was her brother. I wished with all my heart that I had never met any of them.

"I warned you, Mr. Cowan," he said, clenching his fists.

"Dammit," I said. "Get lost, both of you!"

"Why, you — "

"Riley!"

It was Emmaline's voice, sharp and commanding. She had risen and was standing between us.

"Don't blame Mr. Cowan," she said coldly. "It's my fault. I followed him here."

Riley stared down at me for several moments, his

hands clenching and unclenching with suppressed fury. Then, without a word, he turned and stalked away. Emmaline followed him. I watched them leave the park and cross Jefferson Davis Street to the white Chrysler. Martin slid behind the wheel and a moment later they were gone. I was about to look away when I saw another car going in the same direction.

It was my fat man in his blue Chevy.

Monday and Tuesday passed uneventfully except for one minor incident. On Monday afternoon I noticed Detective Wagner tailing me from my office to a client's home and back again. I heard nothing from my Spanish friend. Emmaline and my fat friend had ceased to haunt me. I was hoping that the hiatus was a good sign, but had a feeling that it was only a lull before the storm.

On Wednesday night, after we'd turned off television and were having our snack in the kitchen, Julie finally got into the act.

"What's bothering you, Neil?" she asked, looking at me over her coffee cup.

"Nothing," I said. "Why?"

"You seem — preoccupied."

"It's just your imagination," I said.

"It is not," she said indignantly. "Neil, I'm your wife, and I know your moods like a book. Come on, darling, loosen up and tell mama."

I laughed. "I've told you more over the years than I ever told my mother. You ought to be satisfied."

"It has something to do with John Royal's murder, hasn't it?"

I could feel myself stiffen all over. "What makes you

say that?"

She lowered her eyes, not looking at me. "I've heard some talk." Her voice was soft, barely audible.

A few nights ago Lynn Barton had mentioned gossip.

I said with more harshness than I intended, "You can't believe everything you hear."

Julie's hand came across the table and rested on mine. "I don't pay attention to gossip, Neil," she said earnestly. "You know me better than that. But I'm no child, either. I'm twenty-nine and I've been your wife for eight years. So I know you, darling. Better than you think."

Her words sent a shiver through me. I started to remonstrate, but she waved me to be quiet: "These nightly trips on business, all of which started after you went up to Peacock Hill to see Mr. John Royal. The worried lines in your face, and now this woman in the park."

That remark really jolted me. "What woman in the park?"

"The one you were with on Sunday."

I could feel a nerve jumping under my right eye. "You mean Mrs. Snyder?" I asked. "I met her quite by accident."

"Maybe the meeting was accidental, Neil," she admitted. "But her name wasn't Snyder."

Again I tried to interrupt, and again she shook her head stubbornly. "Don't try lying to me," she said. "Mrs. Royal's picture was in the paper today. Linda saw it and came running to tell me it was the same lady who was 'with Daddy in the park.'"

"Okay, so it was Mrs. Royal. What's the deal?"

"Why was it necessary to lie to your child?"

I shrugged. Julie's eyes were focused on mine remorselessly, crowding me into a corner.

"I don't know," I said finally. "I thought of it on the spur of the moment because I was afraid you'd jump to the wrong conclusions. I know about some of the gossip — I thought you might, too."

Julie played with her spoon. "The other night you made quite a point about my loyalty if I found you'd been playing around," she said. "To use your own words, 'with a nice, luscious redhead.' Emmaline Royal is a blonde. But was it she you had in mind?"

I got to my feet. "Come on, Julie, lay off!" I said angrily. "You're trying to build on something that isn't there."

I went to the sink, washed and dried my cup and saucer, and all the while I could feel her eyes on my back. I wanted to turn around and get down on my knees and bury my face in her lap and beg her forgiveness, but because I was still hoping to keep as much as I could from her, I didn't.

She joined me at the sink. Her eyes were serious and a little sad, I thought. "Neil, remember what I said the other night? I said that whatever happened, I would always love you. I meant it, Neil."

I took her cup and saucer from her and put them in the sink. Then I put my arms around her and drew her close.

"I know you did," I said. "And here's something for you to remember, too. I'll always love you."

That night both of us had trouble trying to fall asleep. Julie tossed and turned. I gritted my eyelids but still I couldn't squeeze myself into unconsciousness. Oddly enough, it wasn't the thought of Emmaline disturbing me. What kept my eyes wide open — and my body — was a fragrance, Julie's fragrance.

Suddenly I seemed to hear my wife cry out. I wasn't sure. The sound could have been the fragment of a sob, or it could have been something out of my own imagination — I might have wanted to believe that Julie needed me, needed me so badly that her emotion caught in her throat and made her moan.

But what came out of that sound — whether it was a real sound or no — was the certainty of my own need, a certainty so real that, when in her restless movements Julie turned once again toward me, I uttered a responding sound — the sound of her name.

"Julie," I murmured. And then I put my mouth softly over her eyes, brushing them.

"Neil," she whispered. "Neil." And she drew down my mouth to hers. "I will always love you. It is true. You do believe me." And with a tender swiftness she led my hand to her warm breast. I felt of its yielding, its firm womanly contours. I stroked the nipple with affectionate fingers, caressed it with the palm of my hand and felt it sweetly grow erect. And then, in tenderness, my hand sought the other breast, fondling and stroking. My wife, I thought. My warm, wonderful wife.

"I believe you, Julie. I believe you will always love me. And you've got to believe me. You've got to," I repeated with desperate intensity. "I love everything that you are, the sound of you, the touch of you — "

"Darling — the touch?"

"Julie. . ."

"Then touch me, husband."

And there was nothing of my Julie, my wife, that I did not touch; and touch by touch she filled my aching hands. Her breasts grew into my turning fingers. Her hips made a warm accommodation to them. Her belly and her thighs reached a remorseless motion under them, and both of our bodies then found a locking and a releasing that, moment by moment, became more heavenly, yet more intolerable.

Yes, we thought we could not kiss each other more, but we did.

We thought we could not clasp each other more tightly, but we did.

We did not think we could draw breaths still wilder, but we did.

We did not think our spines could jacknife us any deeper into the plunges of passion, but they did. They did, and at the bottom-most depth we were a long, lavish growing into each other, a searching for hot union and a finding of it.

I thought, then, my body would burst with the thousand delights of Julie. And it did. Her incandescence exploded all around me into showering bliss.

"I don't want it to stop, I don't want you to go," her words shot into the base of my throat. "Don't stop, don't go, darling, my Neil. Ah, sweet!" She shook her head savagely from side to side on the pillow.

"Julie."

"Yes."

"Julie — "

And the nethermost sound of her ecstasy — and mine — shook us uncontrollably.

In a moment my Julie, my wife, smiled. I had rarely seen such a smile of serenity.

"I told you I love you," she said, and the next second she was sleeping blissfully.

I lay for a long time staring up at the ceiling. Would we — the question went round and round in my brain — would Julie and I have this same oneness of feeling for each other once my affair with Emmaline would be made public? And I was certain that affair would be made public at any moment. I didn't want to lose that mutuality, that sharing of soul, now re-established between Julie and myself. Yes, I deserved to lose it. But — without it — I would be emotionally dead.

About four o'clock I got out of bed and padded softly across the hall into Linda's room. She was holding her favorite doll and there was a smile on her face. I leaned down and kissed her, then I went into the living room to pace and smoke. Peering through the Venetian blinds, I could see halfway down the street. There was a car parked near Howie Evan's house, and it looked like the Dodge I'd seen the other night. I watched it closely for several minutes and, sure enough, I caught a faint flash of light, as if someone were putting a match to a cigarette. Like proverbial postal carriers, Lieutenant Gainey's men let neither rain nor any other meteorological obstacles keep them from their appointed tasks.

CHAPTER TEN

Julie seemed her usual self the next morning, laughing and joking all through breakfast. Maybe she was shamming — studying her uneasily, I couldn't tell. Maybe down deep inside she was eating her heart out. I took my uncertainty with me to the office.

Kathy had a sprightly smile on her face when I walked in. She had two moods — sad when something went wrong with her tempestuous romance with the unpredictable Willie Cahill, exuberant when everything ran smoothly. This morning she was cheerful and I was relieved. I could use a little sunshine the way I felt.

She stood in the doorway with a mischievous look in her eyes as I went through the mail.

"I stood Willie up last night," she said happily.

I looked up absently. "How'd he take it?"

"I don't know. He called three times and I hung up on him every time."

"Good for you."

Her chin came up. "It served him right," she said defiantly. Then her eyes clouded and I could see the doubt creeping in. "I hope your plan works, Mr. Cowan."

I hoped so, too. "It will," I assured her. "Willie's crazy about you."

She went back to her desk humming. I pushed away the mail and resumed my worries about Julie. I had a frightened feeling that she was slipping away from me. Not swiftly like an ebbing wave, but little by little — I might never realize when the final break came. She would try to keep up appearances to the end — how could I fight something I might not be able to see or recognize?

A couple of calls came in around ten o'clock and helped keep my mind off my troubles. A woman over on Loring Place wanted to sell her home and buy a lot in Highland Shores with the money. Houses were not moving too fast at the moment, and I told her she might have to be patient. We sell some houses during the summer months, but we do our best business in fall and winter. She agreed to list the house with me and agreed to a ninety-day contract.

A builder over in Blackwater, a small community about eighteen miles west of Jellico, wanted to get a rundown on property values in Jellico. I drove over and filled him in. His name was Jewett Dakin, a pleasant-faced man in his late thirties.

"Glad you made it today, Mr. Cowan," he said, waving me to a chair. "I understand you sold some Lake Chicopee land recently?"

"That's right. Forty acres in all."

"To the late Mr. Royal?"

"Yes."

"Mind telling me the prices."

"Not at all. The information can be obtained by anyone at the county tax office, but to save you a trip, it was a hundred and twenty thousand dollars."

Dakin nodded. "I thought so. Why, do you suppose, should anyone want to sell the property to me for seventy-five thousand?"

This was news to me. "Who made you the offer?"

"A Mr. Riley Martin."

This was a twist I hadn't figured on. I was no lawyer, but it seemed to me that the Lake Chicopee land, as well as the rest of John Royal's assets, could not be disposed of until the estate was inventoried and checked by the government for inheritance tax purposes. Was Riley Martin panicking? It didn't seem possible. He had been thoroughly checked out by the police. Maybe he was just out for a fast dollar.

"I wouldn't touch it if I were you," I said. I told him about the deed's being in John Royal's name.

Dakin fingered his ear thoughtfully. "He could have signed the papers over to his wife or his brother-in-law before he was killed," he said.

I had to admit the possibility. "I'd check with the Recorder's Office in Jellico if I were you," I said.

He asked me a number of questions about the property and its accessibility to Jellico's downtown shopping district. From his tone it was apparent that he was more than interested. I couldn't blame him. At seventy-five grand the thing was a steal.

After some desultory conversation, Dakin thanked me for my assistance and we shook bands. He promised to look me up when he came to Jellico and I headed back in the Plymouth.

The talk with Dakin gave me plenty of food for thought. Was there something wrong on Peacock Hill? I had gotten the impression from the few times I had seen them together, that Emmaline and her brother did not hit it off too well. If Riley was trying to unload the Lake Chicopee property it could mean a lot — or it could mean nothing. But this new aftermath to John Royal's death was something to keep an eye on.

I was halfway home when the car suddenly went dead. I managed to coast off the highway. I got out, raised the hood and saw that one of the battery cables had come off. I put it back on, but I would need a hammer to make it secure. I opened the trunk compartment and was rummaging, through the tool kit when I noticed a small cloth bundle in a corner, behind the spare tire. I knew instantly that I had never seen it before. Curious, I reached in and unraveled the cloth. My hand shook as I stared down at a shiny, blue-steel revolver.

It was a .32, the same caliber that had killed John Royal.

Despite the midday heat, I felt cold. There was no question that I was looking at the murder gun. Bob Jamieson had been right — someone was out to set me up for John Royal's murder.

A motorist paused on the highway and wanted to know if he could help, but I managed a grin and assured him I was okay. After he was gone, I rewrapped the gun and stuck it in my pocket. I found the hammer and pounded the cable clamp into place. I put the hammer back in the tool kit, closed the trunk and got behind the wheel and settled down to some heavy thinking. The situation called for anything but rashness.

What should I do with the gun? Drive to Gainey's office and give it to him? But what could I say, that I'd found it in my trunk compartment? The average citizen might give me the benefit of the doubt, but a shrewd, case-hardened police officer, never. He would throw the book at me so fast my head would swim. By not turning in the gun I would become guilty of withholding evidence — but anything was better than being charged with murder.

I thought about telling Jamieson, but quickly vetoed the notion. It would be making him an accessory if he helped me dispose of the gun without going to the police — and he might refuse to implicate himself. In any case it wasn't fair to put him on the spot.

My best bet, I finally decided, was to find a safe hiding place for it myself — until events made it possible for me to deliver it to the police.

I looked around at the tall slash pines and the row of Australian pines. Directly across the road from where I was parked was a boarded-up juice stand closed for the summer. It would make a good marker, if and when I decided to come back for the gun. I squashed my cigarette in the tray and walked a short distance into the woods. A slash pine that had almost been seared in two caught my attention. Stooping, I dug a small hole in the soft earth at the base of the tree with my hands. Then I put the bundle into it and covered it up. I patted the ground evenly around it and scattered some leaves and twigs over it.

I straightened and studied my handiwork. It looked safe enough.

I got back in the car and headed once again for Jellico. I kept looking in the rear-view mirror to see if I was being tailed, but the road behind me was empty. My breath took a long time steadying. If it hadn't been for the loose cable clamp, I'd never have known the gun was in the car.

Lieutenant Gainey's car was in my office driveway when I got back. He was sitting on my leather couch, reading a magazine.

He looked up and smiled. "Been on the move, eh?" he said pleasantly enough. But his eyes were probing.

I nodded. "New client in Blackwater," I said. "You can check it. Anything I can do for you, Lieutenant?"

"Yes," he said. He got to his feet. "I'd like to examine your car if you don't mind."

"Certainly. Mind if I ask why?"

"Routine. It won't take long."

We went outside and I watched while he turned the trunk compartment inside out. He checked the front and back seats. When he had replaced them, he took off his coat and donned a grease monkey's smock he got from his own car. Then he eased himself under the car and examined the frame with painstaking thoroughness. He looked under the hood, under the dashboard and in the glove compartment.

His shirt was soaken when he was through. He leaned against the car and wiped his face with a handkerchief and smiled.

"Okay," he said. "Where is it?"

"Where is what?"

"The gun. The one that killed John Royal."

Somehow I managed a grin. "I don't get it, Lieutenant What make you think I have the murder gun?"

He took out a pack of butts, offered me one.

"Let's say a little birdie told me," he said, exhaling. "What'd you do. Mr. Cowan, bury it?"

I couldn't help thinking the guy must be psychic — then I saw him looking at my hands, traces of dirt still clung to them. It came to me that he had offered me a cigarette just to see my hands.

He said, "You ought to have washed up."

I studied my paws. Fortunately, besides the soil particles, there were also grease smudges on my fingers. "I had a little trouble with the car on the trip from Blackwater." I took a deep drag on the cigarette. "I suppose somebody tipped you that the gun was in my car?"

He hesitated a moment before nodding.

"Did it occur to you to wonder how anyone would know. If I were a murderer, would I be so stupid as to let anyone know?"

I could see by the expression in his eyes that he had already given the angle considerable thought.

"You could have had a falling-out with, say, an accomplice," he suggested. "Or you could have been careless. Or somebody might have gotten curious enough, with all the talk that's going around, to make a point of finding out."

"You still think I killed Mr. Royal?"

"Yes."

"Why, because of my affair with Mrs. Royal?"

"That, and one other very important thing," he said. "You're the only person closely associated with the Royals who doesn't have an alibi."

"Have you given any thought to the possibility that Mrs. Royal or her brother could have hired someone to do it?" I asked.

He smiled, dropped the cigarette on the driveway

and put his heel on it. "I've given it a lot of thought, Mr. Cowan," he said. "I've had their movements scrutinized for a month before the murder. You're the only potential suspect either one of them knew during that period." He paused a moment. "Did Mrs. Royal ask you to kill her husband for her?"

He was watching me closely, hoping that the statement would have a devastating effect. It almost did, but I caught myself in time.

"You're a good man, Lieutenant," I said. "But you're wasting your time on me. I did not kill Mr. Royal."

"How about the gun — did you bury it? Where did you get the soil on your hands?"

I shook my head wearily. "I told you — motor trouble. You've been fooling with my car. Look at your own hands."

Bits of my driveway clung to his grease-stained fingers.

He smiled. "Okay — your round. Good day, Mr. Cowan."

Kathy was insatiably curious about Lieutenant Gainey's visit and finally I had to send her on an errand to get her out of my hair. I was alone in the office when the phone rang. I picked up the receiver.

"Meester Cowan?"

My blood pressure jumped fifty points. It was my Spanish friend.

"Yes?" I said.

"This is Señor Raúl Lopez. You must remember me?"

"I remember you," I said harshly. "You're the guy who made a phony appointment with me for Mr. Royal."

"A phony appointment?" He sounded aghast. "I don't follow you, *señor*."

"Mr. Royal didn't want to see me that night, because neither he nor his wife had ever heard of you, Mr. Lopez!"

"But that is ridiculous! I assure you that I made the appointment in good faith." There was a short pause. "Perhaps, if you had kept that date Señor Royal would still be alive."

It was something I didn't like to think about. "Who are you, and what do you want?" I demanded.

"Who I am doesn't matter. But I want to help you, if you will believe me."

"Let's say I believe you," I said. "What's on your mind?"

"There is much talk that the police think you killed Mr. Royal. Is this not so?"

From the way people were talking, I was surprised that my picture wasn't in the post office. "Suppose it is," I said.

"Ah, then I am right! You are under suspicion." There was a long pause, as if he was trying to make up his mind. "Maybe I am sticking my neck out, as you Americans say. But I can help you clear yourself."

"You know who killed Royal?" I asked quickly.

"*Sí.*"

"Why don't you tell the police?"

Señor Lopez chuckled. "Don't be naive, Mr. Cowan. The police and I are not what you would call buddies."

"Then how do you propose to help me?"

He thought it over for several moments. "Can you meet me tomorrow night on Waterfront Street?" he asked.

"I think so."

"There are two canning plants on the north side of the street, between Dial and Jonquil Streets. Do you know where I mean?"

I was familiar with the area and told him so.

"Good! Then meet me at nine o'clock tomorrow night in front of the Hughes Canning plant. And, Mr. Cowan. Bring ten hundred-dollar bills."

"That's a lot of money," I protested.

He laughed. "Is it too high a price to pay to keep you out of the state penitentiary?" he chided. "You will be there at nine o'clock sharp?"

"Yes," I said. "I'll be there."

"With the money?"

"With the money. How do I know you won't double-cross me?"

"You don't. But I assure you, I have no intention of double-crossing you. See you tomorrow night."

He hung up.

My mind was whirling when I replaced the receiver. Whoever and whatever he was, I had to admit that Señor Lopez at least sounded convincing. Although he promised to sell me the name of John Royal's murderer, I wondered how he knew, and why he was willing to tell me. But if his information took me off the hook, I figured a thousand dollars would be a small price to pay.

Linda came running out to meet me when I got home that evening. She had a pretzel in her hand and her eyes were beaming with excitement.

"Daddy, play 'make a wish' with me!" she exclaimed.

I remembered playing the game when I was a kid. Some things never change.

I squatted on my haunches and grinned. "Okay, honey," I said. "Let's go."

She held out the pretzel. "Put your finger through one of the holes, Daddy," she said.

"Okay, how's this?"

"That's fine. Now pull!"

We pulled and I got the biggest part. Disappointment washed over her face for an instant and was gone.

"What'd you wish for, Daddy?" she asked.

I'd wished that things would always be the same at the Cowan home — that nothing, absolutely nothing, would ever interfere with its warm, gentle atmosphere.

But I didn't tell that to Linda. "I wished," I said, picking her up and carrying her into the house, "that you will grow up to be as pretty as Mommy."

Julie was setting the table. She looked at me and smiled. "What a line you've got, Neil Cowan!" she said. "But isn't she a little young for it?"

Julie looked so good and clean that all my feeling for her, all the gratitude for her years of love and understanding, welled up inside me. I put Linda down and took her in my arms and held her close, and some of the urgency inside me flowed through to her, for she clutched me so tightly. And through it all I wondered a little desperately — had there been a touch of coldness, of wariness and suspicion in her question about Linda?

"Mommy, Daddy! Break it up. I'm hungry!" wailed Linda, tugging at her mother's skirt.

Her plaintive appeal broke the spell and we laughed. But I knew more surely than ever that Señor Lopez was right. A thousand dollars was a paltry sum indeed, to pay for keeping whatever happiness still remained to me.

The evening passed outwardly as had so many before it. We had dinner, put Linda to bed, looked at television. Julie seemed her old self, and I began to breathe more easily. The unpleasantness of the night before was apparently forgotten. We had our usual snack and went to bed, and in a matter of moments, Julie was asleep. But my mind was too full to join her in slumber.

I thought about Riley Martin's efforts to sell the land, of finding the gun in my car and Lieutenant Gainey's unsuccessful search for it afterward. Ever since John Royal's murder each of my days seemed a lifetime. Then I thought about my Spanish friend and the information he was going to give me tomorrow night. Maybe, with a little luck, this whole mess would be over in another forty-eight hours.

Around two o'clock I snapped into instant alertness. I heard a stealthy sound on the driveway outside the bedroom window. When it was repeated, I eased out of bed and opened the night table drawer. A metal flashlight makes a substantial weapon. I clutched it in my right hand and tiptoed to the window. The night was hazy, humid, with rain clouds scuttling across a starless sky.

I could see no one, but I knew someone was out there. I listened for several minutes, but there was no further sound. I padded softly into the kitchen, opened the door and slipped onto the side porch. I was beginning to wonder if my imagination had been working overtime when I heard it again. Like the scrape of a shoe on cement — near the garage.

I focused the flashlight toward the sound and flicked it on. The bright beam made everything in its path clear and distinct. A shadow moved on the edge of the light, and I hurried toward it. I could hear him plainly now, but I couldn't see anything because of the other houses and the shrubbery. Then it was too late. The sounds receded, died. Whoever the trespasser was, he had been swallowed up in the darkness.

I checked the lock on the front door. It hadn't been tampered with. And there were no footprints in the dew-damp grass. I went into the house, wondering if my visitor could have been the little fat man.

Julie, her sleep-filled eyes tinged with apprehension, was waiting for me by the side door. "What's the matter, Neil?"

I grinned sheepishly. "I thought I heard somebody prowling around, but it was a false alarm."

"You're sure?"

I put my arm around her shoulder. "Of course, honey. Come on, let's go back to bed."

We lay there a long time, neither of us saying anything. I hoped I had convinced her that I'd only been hearing things. The silence around us was complete, except for the occasional hum of a passing car.

"Neil?"

"Yes?"

"Is Linda in any danger?"

"Of course not! Go to sleep."

Was Linda in danger? I hadn't thought she might be — now I wasn't sure. My hand found Julie's in the dark and I squeezed it reassuringly. There were too many loose threads to my puzzle — suddenly I wasn't sure of anything.

CHAPTER ELEVEN

Before going to the office on Friday morning I drove downtown and picked up ten one-hundred-dollar bills at the bank. Bob Jamieson was going in as I was leaving, and we exchanged a few pleasantries. He wanted to know if anything new had developed since we'd talked last and I told him no.

A North Carolina couple came to my office around ten-thirty. They were looking for a small orange grove with a five or six-room house. I had some dozen listings in this category, and spent most of the day showing them around. The old guy liked several of the places, but his wife turned thumbs down on them all. It was four o'clock when we parted company in front of the office, and all I had gained was the exercise.

Meanwhile the papers had relegated news of the murder to the inside pages. The Tampa *Tribune* hardly mentioned it at all, while the Jellico *Sentinel* gave it less and less coverage each day. There's nothing so dead as an unsolved murder, even if the victim is a John Cameron Royal.

I left for Waterfront Street around eight-thirty. Normally, the drive takes fifteen minutes, but I wanted to be early. I could feel the tension building up inside me, gnawing at me. If Señor Lopez was telling the truth about knowing who killed Royal, I figured on going straight to Lieutenant Gainey with the information. Gainey didn't have to believe me, but I might have something riding on my side for a change.

As I maneuvered the car through the downtown traffic, I considered the possibility of taking Señor Lopez to police headquarters with me. I knew he wouldn't come willingly, but he might not be big enough to say no.

Shops and stores gave way to service stations, a junk yard, run-down rooming houses, small manufacturing plants and warehouses. Waterfront Street was lonely, deserted at night. It parallels the dock area, where a number of fishing craft of various shapes and sizes were moored. Larger boats loomed farther out in the Gulf.

I drove slowly past two canning plants but could see no one. Lopez was probably hiding in some doorway, waiting for me. Or he might be staying out of sight to make sure I had come alone. There was an all-night diner near the corner. I parked near it, switched off my lights, and walked back to the Hughes Canning plant. The two-story building was dark, as was the Pepperill plant next to it. The silence was deep and foreboding, and I was conscious of a tight, jumpy feeling in the pit of my stomach. I had a hunch that my Spanish friend was watching my every move.

After a few minutes, I started walking toward the Pepperill plant. Maybe if I crossed up his instructions I could draw Lopez out. I was passing the alley between the two buildings, when it happened.

Somebody stuck a gun in my back.

"Hold it nice and steady, *amigo*," said a voice that was little more than a sibilant whisper. "Raise the hands and place them on top of the head. But do it slowly. Very slowly."

The muscles in my throat refused to work. I swallowed a couple of times, raised my hands slowly.

"Señor Lopez?"

"Yes."

I shrugged. "Why the gun?"

"Señor Lopez takes no chances, my friend. You came alone?"

"Of course."

"And you brought the money?"

"Yes, I brought it." I started to turn around, but changed my mind when he increased the pressure of the gun in my back.

"Señor Lopez does not wish you to see him," he said.

There was something about the timbre of his voice that bothered me. I had heard it before. Perhaps it was the intonation he gave to some of the words, I don't know. But I had a hunch that Señor Raúl Lopez was not a complete stranger to me.

"The money," he said. "In what denomination did you bring it?"

"Ten one-hundred-dollar bills," I said.

"That is very good. Where do you have it?"

"It's in my inside coat pocket. In an envelope."

He moved the gun up my back until it rested between my shoulder blades. I wanted to laugh. This was the guy I was planning to take to police headquarters, by force, if necessary.

"Now take your left hand down, get the envelope and toss it behind you," he said. "But do it very slowly. *Comprende?*"

I shook my head. "I want the name first."

"You are hardly in a position to argue, my friend.

Please do as I say."

"And if I don't?"

I could hear him sigh. "Then I'm afraid I will have to take it from your dead body," he said ominously.

There was nothing I could do. You can't argue against a gun in your back. I lowered my left arm slowly, reached in, got the envelope and tossed it behind me. I heard it hit the pavement.

"That is good, *amigo*. Very good."

"Now the name," I said.

"Ah, yes. The name. Step backward into the alley. Slowly, please."

Only then did it dawn on me that he wasn't going to give me any name. He was going to kill me and plant enough evidence on me to convince Gainey that I had killed John Royal. I would have to do something fast. Going into that alley would be like signing my death warrant.

I kicked backwards with all my strength, hoping to hit a leg hard enough to disconcert him. But all I hit was air.

But something did hit me. It cracked against the side of my head and I went sprawling across the sidewalk to the curb. Millions of little light bulbs exploded in my brain. From far away I heard someone swearing. This was followed by a searing pain in my side. I knew I was trying to get up, but my hands kept sliding forward as if the sidewalk were an ice rink. My head was full of fuzz, and I tried shaking it.

That was when I saw the headlights coming toward me. I fell on my side, waiting for I knew not what. I could hear footsteps receding hurriedly in the distance, and then the car went by, going in the same direction. It looked like the dark-blue Chevy. Hell, it was the dark-blue Chevy! I lay there helplessly, wanting to shout after it. Shout what? Why did I suddenly think the little fat man wanted to help me? Maybe it was because he had never tried to hurt me. Not actually.

My head began to clear and I staggered to my feet. The street was as empty and silent as a tomb. Lopez was gone, and so was the fat man. I looked around for the envelope, but it, too, was gone.

Bright boy, Cowan. I leaned against the canning plant wall to steady myself, grateful for the cool breeze off the gulf. I was a corker, I was. All anyone had to do was pick up the phone and ask me to bring him a thousand bucks, and by God, I brought it! Nothing cheap about me. And, if that wasn't enough, I get clobbered for good measure.

I could see clearly now. The nauseated feeling I'd had when I got to my feet had passed. I fumbled in my pocket for cigarettes.

A pair of headlights turned the corner and I braced myself against the damp wall. In this neighborhood one could expect almost anything, and there was always a chance that Señor Lopez would return to finish the job.

But it wasn't Señor Lopez. Or the fat man in the blue Chevy. It was a green-and-white police car, and it drew up to the curb in front of me. A tall, young-looking cop got out and played the beam of a flashlight over me.

"What's wrong, buddy?" he asked. He shone the light in my face.

I smiled and shook my head. "Nothing's wrong," I said. Somehow I felt stupid, inadequate.

He leaned down and picked up my Panama and handed it to me. "This yours?" he asked.

"Yes." I took it and put it on my head. I wondered if the back of my head was bleeding.

"You been drinking?"

"No."

He shined the light in my eyes. "What happened?" he asked again.

"I was passing this alley when I was hit on the back of the head," I said. "Don't ask me who did it. I didn't see him."

He examined the back of my head. "It's swollen," he said. "But the skin isn't broken."

Hard-headed Cowan, that's me. "I'll be all right," I said. "That's my car down the street."

A second cop came out of the car. He was shorter than the first one, and much older.

"Did he get anything?" he asked.

I pretended to check my possessions. "No, I've got everything. Something must have scared him off."

The older cop took a memorandum book from his hip pocket. "What's your name?" he asked.

"Neil Cowan. I live at two-twelve Maple Street. I'm in the real estate business here in Jellico."

The cop wrote it down. "And you don't know what the guy looks like?"

"No, I'm sorry to say."

They searched the alley with their flashlights but, outside of a few cigarette butts, could find nothing. Then they walked with me to my car. I slid behind the wheel.

"Sure you can drive?" the older cop asked.

"I'm sure," I said, starting the engine. "And thanks."

They nodded and went back to their car. I made a right turn on Dial Street and decided to go to the office to check my appearance. I didn't want to go home looking like I'd been in a pier six brawl. Julie had enough on her mind as it was.

The moment I switched on the overhead light in the outer office I knew that somebody had been looking for the envelope Lynn Barton had entrusted to me. The room was a wreck. Desk drawers had been removed and their contents strewn everywhere. The leather couch and the two leather chairs had been slashed and turned over. The pictures hung awry on the walls. The mess in my office was even worse. The marauder had removed the drawers from the file cabinets, and the data and records kept in the folders were scattered over the room. A hurricane couldn't have done a more thorough job.

I took the pencil flashlight and went into the lavatory. I snapped on the overhead light, got down on my knees and focused the beam into the narrow aperture between the tank and the wall.

The envelope was gone.

I got to my feet and slumped against the wall. I was tired and discouraged. I'd failed both myself and Lynn Barton. After a few minutes of self-recrimination, I studied myself in the cabinet mirror. There wasn't a mark on me and my clothes were okay. Outside of the bump on my head and damage to my ego, I was as good as new.

But how had he got in? I checked the door and the windows in the outer office without finding any signs of a forced entry. But the screen in the rear window of my office had been cut. None of the panes was broken, which meant I had forgotten to lock the window before leaving that afternoon.

It took me over an hour to straighten the two rooms. The file folders were the hardest to put together, and took most of my time. Finally, when everything was more or less in order, I thought about Lynn Barton. She should know about the envelope. I checked my wristwatch. It was ten minutes to eleven.

I dialed her number. The phone rang, but no one picked it up. I hung up and dialed again. There was always a chance I had dialed wrong the first time. The phone rang and again nobody lifted the receiver. A cold, fluttery feeling came into my stomach.

I hung up and realized I was shaking. Maybe she was out somewhere — possibly she had gone to a movie. I didn't really believe she had, but thinking about the possibility made me feel better. I sat there until eleven-ten and tried again. Still no answer. I even called Information and asked for her number, on the chance that I had written it down wrong. It was the number I was calling.

It was no use — I had to do something. I locked the office, got in the car and drove to the Brighton Apartments. There was a row of brass letterboxes in the vestibule, with nameplates below them and small ivory buttons. There was no answering buzz.

I pressed another button and the door purred open at my touch. I hurried to the second floor and tried

Lynn's door. It was locked. I put my ear against the door and listened, but there was no sound. My mind began conjuring up all kinds of possibilities, all bad.

There was only one thing to do — find the superintendent and get him to open the door. I hurried back downstairs. A metal sign over the letterboxes said he lived in apartment 1C, in the south wing. I went across the courtyard and rang his bell.

After several moments a stocky man in his early fifties opened the door. He was barefoot and shirtless, and the expression on his heavy-jowled face told me he wasn't exactly pleased with the intrusion.

"I've been trying to get in touch with Miss Barton in Two B," I said. "She doesn't answer and I'm worried."

He scratched his stomach and suppressed a yawn, all in the same motion. "Maybe she's out," he said irritably.

"But I've been calling her since early in the evening," I lied. "I had an appointment."

My worried expression finally thawed him out. "Whaddaya want me to do about it?" he complained. "I can't go barging in there at this hour of the night."

"Something may have happened to her," I said. "She could be sick, helpless. If you won't do something about it, maybe the police will."

That did it. "No need to bother the cops about this." He shook his head resignedly. "Okay. I'll get the key and go with you."

He slipped into shoes and a shirt. Before putting the key in Lynn's lock, he pressed the button outside her door several times.

"She could have come back while you were talking

to me," he said.

When there was no answer, he keyed open the door and we went inside. He thumbed on the light switch. There was complete silence in the apartment.

The super looked at me and shrugged. "Miss Barton?" he called.

There was no answer, and I had a strange feeling that there wasn't going to be any answer.

"Miss Barton?" he called again. We went into the living room and then the bedroom. Everything was neat and in its proper place. I breathed a little easier. I'd been expecting signs of a struggle, bloodstains, anything. Even a body.

I went into the kitchen while he checked the bathroom. Everything seemed in order. There was a key on the utility table and absent-mindedly I picked it up. It looked like a duplicate of the key the super had used to get in the apartment. If it was a key to the apartment, why hadn't Lynn Barton taken it with her?

Without knowing why, I dropped it into my pocket. I went into the bedroom, where I found the super inspecting the clothes closet.

"Find anything?" I asked.

He turned and faced me, a puzzled frown on his face. "That's funny," he said.

"What is?"

"When I rented the apartment to her about a month ago, I carried two suitcases upstairs." he said. "There's only one in the closet. And from the looks of the hangers, she's taken some of her clothes with her."

I joined him by the closet. He was right. Nearly half

the clothes hangers were empty. I took the pencil flashlight and played it around the closet. A brown leather briefcase stood in a corner behind the suitcase. A name was embossed on it. I stooped over and peered more closely — the name wasn't Lynn Barton. It was Lois Bowman.

Was she using a phony name?

I closed the closet door and went back to the living room. The super followed me, looking worried.

"Think we oughta call the cops?"

I shook my head. "I don't think so. She may have decided to go out of town for a few days. I've been stood up before. I was just worried she might be ill — but obviously she's simply out."

He looked relieved. "Yeah. Okay, let's close up. I need my shuteye. I'm beat."

We were almost to the door when the phone rang. The super looked at me and I looked at him, indecision in our faces.

"Better see who it is," I said. "It may be important." He nodded, went to the end table and picked up the receiver. "Yeah. . . . no, she isn't here . . . I'm the superintendent. . . . No, I haven't seen her in a couple of days. . . . I don't know where she is . . . what? . . . . No, I'm not one of her boy friends. Who is this? . . . . Oh, yeah? . . . . Well, the same to you and many of 'em . . . G'bye!"

He slammed the receiver.

"Whaddaya think of a crumb like that?" he said, shaking his head. "He wanted to know if I was one of her boy friends. Imagine a dame like her even givin' me a second look!" I went out in the hall and waited while he made sure the door was locked. He kept shaking his head.

"Talkin' to me like that," he said. "And him a foreigner!"

I looked at him searchingly. "A foreigner?"

"Yeah. Sounded like Spanish, the crumb."

I left him to get his shuteye, went back to my car and did some thinking. It was obvious to me that Lynn Barton — or Lois Bowman — had flown the coop. She had impressed me as a woman with some nerve, so she must have had a very good reason for lighting out without letting me know. But what worried me most was that Lopez had her telephone number. Could they be working together at some subtle game I didn't understand? Try as I might, I couldn't make myself believe that. Lopez was a thief.

Thinking of Raúl Lopez reminded me of the feeling I'd had tonight when I heard him for the first time off the phone. His voice had had a familiar timbre — but I still didn't place it.

It was getting late. Julie would be in bed. I started the car and headed home. The house was dark when I swung into the driveway. I was locking the garage door when I heard voices. Julie was on the porch talking to someone.

I went around to the front of the house and onto the porch. Julie's guest was a man. Lieutenant Gainey.

CHAPTER TWELVE

I paused, frozen with shock and anger. I looked at Julie. A sliver of moonlight filtered through the porch screen, illuminating her face. She was smiling a little anxiously.

"This is Lieutenant Gainey, Neil," she said. "He claims you had some trouble on Waterfront Street tonight."

My pulse rate slowed down. Gainey must have read the report turned in by the two officers. I stuck out my hand as though meeting him for the first time.

"Glad to know you, Lieutenant," I said.

We shook hands. His face was expressionless.

"Care to tell me about it, Mr. Cowan?"

I pulled over a porch chair. "Let's all sit down," I said. "I'm bushed. There isn't much I can tell you, Lieutenant. I was down on Waterfront Street waiting for a client when somebody slugged me. Mugger, probably. Fortunately, he didn't get anything. I think the headlights of the police car scared him off."

"You didn't see him?"

"No. He hit me from behind." That much at least was true.

"How do you feel, Neil?" Julie asked quickly. "Should we get a doctor?"

I grinned and shook my head. "No. But I'll probably have a headache in the morning."

"Whom were you supposed to meet, Mr. Cowan?" asked Gainey.

"Somebody named William Riker. He phoned and said he was interested in commercial waterfront property. Only time he could meet me was after hours. He mentioned a substantial amount of money, so I was interested. Of course," I added as an afterthought, "the name could have been phony. He said he was from out of town."

"Do you suppose he was the man who hit you?" Gainey's voice was dripping with skepticism.

"I don't even know if it was a man that hit me. Could have been a woman. Or a chimpanzee."

We sat in silence for several minutes. Gainey was beginning to fidget when the stillness was shattered by a loud wail from inside the house.

Julie jumped to her feet. "Linda must be having a bad dream," she said. "Please excuse me, Lieutenant."

Gainey got to his feet and nodded. After Julie went inside he took a pack of cigarettes from his pocket and again offered me one. It was too dark, this time, for him to see my shaking hands.

"Walk with me to the car, Mr. Cowan?"

I accompanied him to the unmarked police car parked a few doors down the street. He opened the door and eased behind the wheel.

"Thanks for not telling Julie," I said. "I appreciate it."

"I didn't do it for you," he said gruffly. "I did it for your wife and kid." He shook his head. "I don't think you know how lucky you are."

"I'm finding out."

"A lot of people do — after they get in trouble. What are you up to?" he asked.

"I don't know what you mean."

His hard eyes gleamed. "Look, Mr. Cowan. Let me assure you that you aren't fooling anybody. Police work is my business just as real estate is yours. We know all the answers as well as all the dodges and finally we always hit the right combination. On the night John Royal was killed, you said you went to Michael Swain's house. But because he was conveniently out of town, there was no way to prove anything. Tonight you have an appointment with a William Riker and he doesn't show up, either." He eyed me speculatively. "Whom did you kill tonight, Mr. Cowan?"

My back was up. I was mad. "I didn't kill Royal," I said hotly. "Nor did I kill anyone tonight. Instead I nearly got killed. If it makes a difference to you, there was no William Riker. The man who called me had a Spanish accent. I didn't want to worry Julie by getting into a discussion with you back in the house."

"Raúl Lopez, the man you told me about?"

"Yes. He said he knew who killed Royal and that he would sell me the killer's name for a thousand bucks."

"And you fell for it?" he asked incredulously.

I shrugged. "Believe it or not, I did."

"He got the thousand dollars?"

"Yes."

"Why didn't you come to me when he phoned?"

"I had no reason to believe you wanted to help me."

His angry silence was eloquent even in the darkness. I could feel it without seeing him. At last he said, "I'm not interested in helping you or anyone else. All I want is the killer. If you're innocent, we're automatically on the same side of the fence. You'd better start praying we don't find a body floating in the bay with your thousand dollars on him." He paused, added: "Good night, Mr. Cowan."

I watched his taillights disappear around the corner before going into the house. Linda had fallen asleep again, and Julie was waiting for me in the bedroom.

"Is something going on that I should know, Neil?" she asked, slipping off her robe and getting into bed.

I hung my coat in the closet, took off my tie, unbuttoned my shirt. "Yes, there is something you should know, honey," I said. I sat on the edge of the bed. "There's been something all along you should've known. But I can't tell you now."

She reached for my hand and held it. "All right, Neil. Can I help?"

I shook my head. "There's only one thing you can do, Julie. Trust me."

She bit her lip, nodded. "All right, Neil. Tell me when you're ready."

Before I left for the office the next morning, Julie reminded me about the bi-monthly dance being held at the Jellico Yacht Club that evening. It was a Chamber of Commerce affair, and while I didn't particularly care about going — I don't even own a rowboat — Julie had been looking forward to it.

"I'll be home early," I promised.

I was kept busy all morning talking to a couple of people who wanted to invest their money in first mortgages. I do very little of this sort of business, and, frankly, don't care for it. I ended up by sending them to a friend of mine who is a specialist.

Kathy had left for lunch a few minutes before Bob Jamieson called.

"Have some trouble last night, Neil?" he asked.

"How did you know?" The way news traveled in a town the size of Jellico was beginning to amaze me.

"I was in Hooks' office a little while ago when Gainey called him. I could tell by Wilbur's answers that something had happened. What was it, Neil?"

I told him about Lopez' call and my subsequent meeting with him on Waterfront Street. I also brought him up to date on Gainey's visit to my home.

"Lopez got away with your money?"

"Yes. There wasn't anything I could do about it, Bob. He had a gun in my back."

"You should have let Gainey know the moment Lopez hung up." Bob sounded mad. "He would have closed off the whole area. With Lopez in custody, Gainey would know a lot more than he does now."

"We're only second-guessing, Bob," I said wearily. "Besides, I was anxious to get off the hook."

We tossed it back and forth for a few minutes before hanging up. But he made me promise not to make any such moves in the future without first talking to him. Bob is a nice guy, as I said, probably because he believes in playing the game according to the rules. I was convinced that sticking to the book was not going to solve John Royal's murder. Whoever had engineered it was as ruthless as he was clever, and no ordinary maneuvers were going to trap him.

I was about to close the office for the day when I happened to put my hand in my pocket and feel something metallic. It was the key I'd found in Lynn Barton's apartment last night. I had a sudden impulse to go back there and look around without the prying eyes of the super watching me, if the key worked. Thought of the briefcase in the closet decided me.

I drove to the Brighton Apartments, parked a block away and went upstairs to 2B. The key opened the door and I went in. Everything seemed just as I had seen it last night. The drapes were drawn and I switched on the light. The place had an unlived-in feeling. I went into the bedroom, got the briefcase and returned to the living room.

I scaled my hat onto an armchair and sat down. I pulled the zipper and dumped the contents on the couch. There were some papers and a couple of snapshots, but not much of anything, really. I examined the papers.

The first one was a birth certificate made out for a Lois Ann Bowman. She was born on December 11, 1925, which made her thirty-three years old. The birthplace was Muncie, Indiana. Her mother's name was Mary Elizabeth and her father is James Joseph.

The next one was a decree of divorce granted to Lois Anne Bowman Duff from Samuel Clyde Duff. It was signed in Vincennes, Indiana, on October 10, 1956. I put it on top of the birth certificate and picked up one of the snapshots. It showed a tall, slim woman and a taller, handsome man. They were wearing bathing suits, and the woman was undoubtedly Lynn Barton. So the two were the same. There were no names or dates on the photo, but I had a hunch the guy was her ex-husband.

The next snapshot was a four-by-five, and showed three people sitting at a table in a nightclub. The three were Lois Bowman, Emmaline Royal and Riley

Martin. All three were smiling. There were glasses on the table and what looked like a magnum of champagne in an ice bucket.

I stared at the picture and frowned. Lois Bowman had admitted knowing Emmaline and her brother, so seeing them together was no surprise. But why had she come to Jellico using a phony name? I turned the picture over and noticed the date: New Year's Eve, December 31, 1955.

Whatever had happened to make her hate Emmaline and her brother had occurred in the past three years. Had she and Martin become involved in some kind of a scandal? Or was Riley Martin — and I was really reaching for this one — really Samuel Clyde Duff?

The possibility excited me. It could account for the hate I'd seen in Lois Bowman's — or Lynn Barton's — eyes. Still, it didn't have to. Women may dislike or loathe a man they were once married to; they may even hate him. But not always.

I shook my head and examined the next piece of paper. It was a graduation certificate issued by Sarah Lawrence College in New York to Lois Ann Bowman in June, 1948. I found a couple of letters from a girl named Beverly. They were postmarked San Diego, California and dated August 2 and 24, 1956. In the first one, Beverly expressed deep shock and sorrow at learning of the sudden demise of Lois' father. While suicide wasn't specifically mentioned, it was implied.

I finished reading the first letter and was about to toss the second aside when I saw something that gave me a start. Near the end of the letter, Beverly wrote:

... I don't see what an open window has to do with your dad's death, Lois. If he shot and killed himself as the police think, what can the window possibly have to do with it? Please try to erase what has happened from your mind and concentrate on making a whole new life for yourself ...

I checked the date on the divorce paper again. October 10, 1956. Only months after the death of her father. Was there any connection between the two events? And what about the open window? What part did it play, if any, in her father's death? There had been an open window in John Royal's den the night he was murdered. Coincidence, perhaps.

I went through the rest of the papers without finding anything that would help me. I was putting them back in the briefcase when I heard a faint click, like the stealthy closing of a door. My hackles rose and I looked around furtively. From where I sat I could see the foyer and part of the kitchen, and the two doors that led into the bedroom and the bathroom.

I investigated and found no one else in the apartment. There was a door to the left of the breakfast nook. I opened it and found myself on a narrow landing. A flight of cement steps led down to the yard. Another flight rose to the third — and top — floor. I went up slowly, one step at a time until I could see around the bend of the stairwell. It was empty.

I returned to the apartment and checked the lock on the kitchen door. It had an automatic latch and showed no signs of tampering. I retrieved the briefcase from the living room and returned it to the closet.

It was only minutes before two o'clock and I had time. I checked the apartment thoroughly for some clue to Lois Bowman's whereabouts. I found none. It began to look as if she had left of her own volition. But then maybe she hadn't. Persuasion can take many forms.

The Yacht Club was ablaze with lights as I swung into Bayshore Drive shortly after eighty-thirty that evening. The building was situated on a strip of land that juts out into the gulf. Tall palms surrounded it. The grounds were beautifully landscaped and the tropical shrubbery was illuminated by soft, amber lights. A driveway curved around the club to the rear where a couple of hundred cars were parked. Music floated out to us on the warm night air.

Julie was lovely, her eyes glowing with anticipation. She caught my look of approval and smiled.

"It's like old times, Neil," she said breathlessly.

"Yes. We must do this more often."

I found a spot between two Chryslers, and one of them, I saw with a start, was Emmaline's. I had completely overlooked the possibility that she might be here tonight. Then, I realized that people don't go into mourning the way they used to.

The dance floor was crowded as we entered through the french doors. I recognized many of the men and women — but there was no use kidding myself, I was looking for Emmaline. She was here, somewhere, and I had a feeling we'd meet before the evening was over.

Julie and I had several dances before going to the bar. The booths were only partially filled. We ordered martinis, and were still nursing them when Bob and Nancy Jamieson joined us briefly.

While the women were busy telling each other how wonderful they looked, Bob gave me the questioning eye. I smiled reassuringly, and he nodded, pleased.

After they left, Julie and I finished our drinks and returned to the dance floor. Julie loved to dance and I wanted her to enjoy herself to the hilt.

During a waltz Mike Swain cut in. I had used Mike in my alibi for the night of John Royal's murder though he didn't know it. His wife always attended whatever get-togethers Mike patronized, but she did not dance and Mike frequently cut in and advanced with his friends' wives.

I went out on the terrace and lit a cigarette. It was a beautiful night, and just breathing the flower-scented air made me feel glad to be alive. For a few moments at least, my troubles were forgotten, and I mentally thanked Julie for making me come.

There was a light step behind me and I turned to see Emmaline. She was a vision in a black evening sheath that accented every curve of her body.

"Hello, Neil."

I nodded, held out the pack of cigarettes. She took one, tapped it on a lacquered nail before letting me light it.

"I didn't think you'd be here tonight," I said.

"You mean because of John?" When I nodded, she smiled. "You know how I felt about him. Regardless of what else I might be, I'm no hypocrite." She paused. "Is Julie with you?"

I nodded, rested my elbows on the wrought-iron railing. "She's dancing," I said.

She slid closer. "Does she know — about us?"

"No."

Emmaline exhaled gratefully. "I'm glad."

We studied the moonlit waters of the Gulf for several minutes without saying anything.

"Has Gainey bothered you lately?" she asked.

"He hasn't let up."

She stomped her foot angrily. "The fool!" she said furiously. "I told him you were nowhere near Peacock Hill that night."

This was news to me. "He questioned you?"

"Of course." She smiled wryly. "You think I'm immune? I'm a suspect, too. Gainey seems to think I had it done and you fit the picture."

Something bothered me. "Did you tell him about our date that night?" I asked.

"I had to, Neil," she said. "You'd admitted our affair. That gave him a lever and I had to be honest with him. I told him I'd made a date with you and broken it without letting you know."

"Did he believe you?"

"No. He said I was trying to cover up for you."

"I don't blame him," I said bitterly. "I'd already told him a different story. My lying convinces him I'm his man."

She placed her hand on mine. "I'm sorry, Neil. I didn't know how much you'd told him."

"I'm not blaming you."

We were so preoccupied with each other that we didn't hear Julie come on the terrace. She was standing beside us before we realized it.

Her eyes fastened on Emmaline. "This, I'm sure, must be Mrs. Royal," she said, smiling.

My stomach was full of butterflies as I introduced them.

"Neil has spoken so much of you," Emmaline said. "Now I can see why. He is a very lucky man."

"Thank you." Julie slipped her hand into mine. She seemed to be trying to tell me something — and presently I knew what. Lew Gainey and Max Wagner approached us and their faces were grim. Something was wrong, and an icy hand clutched my heart. They were not dressed for the dance — they were obviously on duty.

Gainey nodded to the two women and looked at me. "You're under arrest, Mr. Cowan," he said quietly. "We're taking you to headquarters."

Julie paled and her fingers tightened on mine. "You can't be serious, Lieutenant," she said huskily.

"You'd better be absolutely sure you know what you're doing," said Emmaline. Her face was flushed with anger.

Gainey smiled. "I always know what I'm doing, Mrs. Royal," he said.

"What's the charge, Lieutenant?" I asked.

"Murder."

Julie gasped and I held her tightly.

"I did not kill John Royal," I told Gainey.

"Who said anything about John Royal?" said Gainey. "I'm arresting you for the murder of Zack Tully."

"Zack Tully?" I gaped at him. "Now I know you're crazy. Who the hell is Zack Tully?"

CHAPTER THIRTEEN

The ride to headquarters was a nightmare. Wagner drove while Gainey and I sat in back. None of us said anything as we headed down Bayshore Drive. I kept asking myself who is, or was, Zack Tully? I had never heard the name before, and as far I knew, I'd never met him. We were turning into Second Street when it suddenly hit me. Could Tully be the little fat man?

Wagner found an empty spot in front of police headquarters and cut the engine. He was getting out of the car when Gainey stopped him.

"Hold it, Max," he said. He turned to me. "What can you tell us about Zack Tully?" he asked.

I shook my head. "As far as I know, Lieutenant, I've never met or heard of the man in my life," I said.

"I figured you'd say that," he said, shaking his head. "Take us to the morgue, Max."

Wagner got back in the car and headed for the Hayman General Hospital a couple of blocks away, on Oakland Street. It was long past visiting hours when we drove into the huge parking lot and most of the windows were dark. Wagner parked the car and we got out and went in a side entrance that had the sign, county morgue, over the door.

We went down a long corridor with whitewashed walls and into a dimly-lit combination waiting room and office. The room contained two long wooden benches, a scarred desk and several filing cabinets. A short, bald-headed old man with thick-lensed glasses peered up at us from behind the desk as we walked in.

"We're back again, old-timer," Gainey said. "What's the number of that guy we found on the waterfront?"

"Eighteen," said the old man.

Wagner and I followed Gainey into a large, cheerless room that smelled of formaldehyde. It was so cold I shivered — partly, perhaps, at the prospect of looking at a dead man. A man I was supposed to have slain.

There was a long row of drawers, resembling huge filing cabinets, on either side of the room. Gainey went to one of them and pulled it open. A body lay on a metal runner, covered by a clean white sheet. He flipped aside the part that shielded the face. There was a neat little bullet hole over the left eye, and his features looked younger and more composed, but I recognized the flabby face immediately.

It was the little fat man.

Gainey's eyes were boring holes through me. "Recognize him now?"

I figured my only chance was to bluff it out. "I never saw him before in my life."

Gainey pushed the drawer back into its receptacle. I could tell he was boiling mad.

"Okay, let's go," he snapped.

We went back to headquarters. Gainey's office was on the second floor, a good-sized room with comfortable chairs, a couch and a neatly kept desk. An air conditioning unit was attached to one of the windows. Gainey waved me to a chair and turned to Wagner.

"Send Benny in," he said. "Then get us some coffee."

I sat with my legs crossed while we waited for Benny.

Gainey stood by the window, looking out and saying nothing.

When Benny showed up, he had a stenotype machine with him. He set it down on a small table, flexed his fingers and looked at Gainey expectantly.

Gainey turned and sat down. His face was set in grim lines and a sliver of apprehension ran up my back. This was it. The showdown. From now on we played for keeps.

"All right, Mr. Cowan," he said quietly. "Let's get down to business. You still say you never saw Zack Tully before tonight?"

"Yes."

Gainey opened a drawer, took out an envelope. He lifted the flap and took out ten one-hundred-dollar bills. My thousand bucks.

"We found this on Tully's body," he said. "It's a thousand dollars. Your thousand dollars. But just to make sure, I questioned the teller at your bank who gave you the money. They keep a record of the serial numbers on denominations of this size. The serial numbers on these bills check with the ones you were given yesterday morning."

I didn't say anything because there was nothing to say. Gainey looked at me steadily. "Still say you didn't know him?"

"Yes."

He flipped a switch on the intercom. "Send Jennings in here," he said.

We waited several moments in silence. Benny's fingers were quiet. I wondered who the hell Jennings was.

The door opened and a white-haired man with a leathery face walked in. He had a battered Panama in his hands. I could feel my heart stop. He was the old guy on Rumar Road who had helped me to my feet.

"Mr. Jennings," said Gainey. "Take a look at this man. Take a good look at him, and tell me if you've ever seen him before."

Jennings looked at me and grinned. "Sure, Lieutenant, that's the man who was mugged the other night on Rumar Road," he said. He turned to me. "How's the head, son?"

I stared down at my clasped hands and said nothing. A lie will get you only so far and no further, and this was the end of the line.

"And that man you saw in the morgue a little while ago is the same man who attacked Mr. Cowan, here?" asked Gainey.

"Yes, sir, that was him, all right." Jennings looked proudly. "I never forget a face."

"Thank you. Mr. Jennings," nodded Gainey. "We'll keep in touch with you."

Jennings went out. Gainey made a steeple of his hands and said nothing for several moments. I had a feeling that he had the *coup de grace* up his sleeve somewhere.

"It looks like your denials are pretty silly," he said.

"I didn't kill Zack Tully, or whatever his name is."

"But you do admit knowing him?"

"No, unless he's the man with the Spanish accent, I've never spoken to him in my life," I said.

"But you have seen him before?" pressed Gainey.

"Yes. He's been following me around Jellico for the past several weeks." I shook my head. "Don't ask me why, because I don't know. The other night on Rumar Road I finally caught up with him. I wanted to make him tell me why he was tailing me, but he got away. I haven't seen him since, until tonight."

"And you don't know anything about him?"

"That's right."

"Well, let me enlighten you," Gainey said. "Zack Tully was an ex-con. His home was in Corry Heights, about ten miles from here, and he made an illegitimate living selling guns." He looked at me closely. "Does that refresh your memory?"

"No. I've never bought a gun in my life."

Gainey sighed. "You know, Mr. Cowan, when the Royal case broke and I first learned about you, I was sympathetic. I figured you had made the same mistake a lot of us would have made if we'd been in your shoes. Emmaline Royal is a beautiful woman. But then you lied to me. Not once, but many times. I don't like liars, not even — "

"Not even when they're trying to save themselves from a bum rap?" I interrupted harshly.

"Not even then," he snapped. "Raiford is full of innocent men. If you don't believe me, you can go up there and ask them yourself." He opened a desk drawer, took out a gun and placed it on the blotter before him.

My heart stood still. It looked like the gun I'd buried in the woods a couple of days ago.

"Ever see this before?" he asked.

I swallowed hard and shook my head.

"That's funny," he said. "It has your prints all over it."

"That's a lie!" I shouted. "I never touched it before I — " I tried to halt the damaging admission, but it was too late.

"Before you buried it? Isn't that what you were going to say?"

I felt like a rank amateur trying to cross swords with a professional. It was no contest.

"Yes," I nodded wearily. "Before I buried it."

"When did you buy it from Tully?"

"I didn't buy it from anybody. I found it in the trunk compartment of my car on my way back from Blackwater on the day you questioned me. I buried it because I had a feeling it was the gun that killed John Royal and I thought I was being framed."

"Very astute reasoning, Cowan," Gainey said. "And do you also know that it's the same gun that killed Zack Tully?"

That knocked me over, but good. I had buried the gun on Thursday morning. Yet Tully had been killed more than twenty-four hours later with the same gun. It was unbelievable. Despite the air conditioning, I was sticky with sweat.

Gainey got up, walked around the desk and glared down at me. "Okay, Cowan, spill it!" he demanded.

He had shed the kid gloves. His eyes told me he was through playing guessing games.

So I told him the whole thing. Everything. From the moment John Royal summoned me to Peacock Hill until he picked me up that evening. I left out nothing, including Lois Bowman and the letter she'd asked me to save for her. I even told him about the favor Emmaline had asked me to do.

He listened quietly, attentively, and all the while the only sound in the room besides my voice was the gentle tapping Benny made with the stenotype keys. It wasn't a long story, and I talked fast, but I thought I'd never get to the end.

When I finished, Gainey just sat there, thinking. He did not look impressed. I found a pack of cigarettes in my pocket, shook one loose and lit it. I felt better. At last the whole truth was out.

"This Lynn Barton or Lois Bowman," he said, finally. "You don't know where she is?"

"No."

"And you don't know what was in that envelope?"

"No."

He slapped the desk impatiently. "You know, Cowan, you're the damnedest guy I ever came across," he said. "On the night of John Royal's murder, your alibi was a man who had conveniently left town. Then, last night, when Zack Tully was murdered, you were alone in your office for nearly two hours. No corroborating witnesses, nothing. Now you inject another woman into the case and she can't be found either."

"I've told you the truth," I said.

"I'll bet," he said. He stared morosely at the wall behind me.

I exhaled deeply. "How did you find the gun?"

"I had a tip," he said. "The caller said he saw you burying the gun early this morning."

"But I put it there Thursday, just before I returned to the office and found you waiting for me," I said.

"You noticed the dirt on my hands."

Wagner returned at this point with several containers of hot coffee. We sat and smoked and drank coffee for several minutes in silence. Then it started again. Gainey questioned me for nearly two hours without a break. He was hoping I'd confess to Tully's, if not John Royal's murder. But I had nothing to confess, and I kept telling him so.

It was after one a.m. when the intercom buzzed. The desk sergeant downstairs said, "Bob Jamieson is here, Lieutenant. He claims he's Mr. Cowan's lawyer."

"Okay, send him up," said Gainey. He flipped the switch. "You've got one of the best, Cowan. But you'll need more than Bob Jamieson to get you out of this one."

Jamieson came in, his somber eyes more serious than ever. He was still wearing evening clothes, as I was. He looked at Gainey, then at Benny and his little machine and finally at me.

"He been giving you a rough time?" he asked.

"It's been a ball," I said.

"What are you going to do, Lieutenant?" he asked Gainey.

"I'm signing a warrant, charging him with first degree murder."

Jamieson nodded. "Mind if I talk with my client alone?"

Gainey hesitated, then shrugged. He looked at Benny and motioned the police stenographer to follow him. Benny picked up his machine and the two men left the room.

Jamieson went to the lieutenant's desk and checked

the intercom. "Just playing it safe," he explained. "Gainey's pretty cute, and I wouldn't put it past him to listen in."

After we'd lit cigarettes, Jamieson asked, "What did you tell him, Neil?"

"Everything," I said. I told him the same story I'd told Gainey. It didn't sound one bit better the second time around.

"He's got a good circumstantial case," he said when I finished. "But that's all it is, circumstantial."

"Finding my money on Tully's body sounds pretty convincing to me," I said.

"You were hit on the head last night, remember?" he said. "What's more, we have two reports turned in by those cops to prove it." He paused to flick some ashes into a tray.

"How is Julie?" I asked anxiously.

"She's holding up fine," he assured me. "I would have been here sooner, but Nancy and I left the dance early to visit a friend. Julie had a time locating me. By the way, you're getting my services for free."

Like all good lawyers, Bob gets steep fees. "How come?" I asked.

He grinned. "Mrs. Royal has retained me to defend you. And according to her, the sky's the limit."

Bob left after advising me not to say anything further to Gainey. He promised to see me later that morning and bring some suitable clothes.

After Jamieson left, Gainey booked me on a suspicion-of-murder charge, then took me to the identification room where I was fingerprinted and photographed, full face and profile. Later, I turned my belongings over to a property clerk and was taken to a cell in the basement.

I was glad to have a cell to myself, for it gave me a chance to do some uninterrupted thinking. I stretched out on the bunk. Whoever had framed me had done an excellent job. If there was a slip-up anywhere, I couldn't find it. Some time during the early hours of the morning I fell into a troubled sleep.

A guard woke me for breakfast. Bob Jamieson showed up around eleven o'clock with some fresh clothes. Because it was Sunday, he had been unable to file his petition for a writ with Circuit Judge Carleton E. Maitland. Bob advised me to sit tight until he could complete arrangements for my bail.

He left some magazines, but I was in no mood for reading. The cell block was almost empty, and it was quiet. I spent most of the day trying to find some flaw in the frame against me, probing the remotest possibilities without coming up with a single lead. Gainey had me cold, and there wasn't anything I could do about it.

Gainey and Wagner came for me around ten o'clock Monday morning and took me to the ground-floor office of Justice of the Peace Duane Kells. A large crowd had gathered in the hall. I'd sold some property for Duane about a year ago and knew that our meeting this way was just as embarrassing for him as it was for me. Bob Jamieson was there and nodded to me when I entered.

Lieutenant Gainey formally presented the warrant. Kells read it carefully. Then, not looking at me, he ordered me held without bail pending action by the

Hummock County grand jury.

As we were leaving, Jamieson joined me. "I've applied for a writ, Neil," he said. "Judge Maitland will act on it in a day or so."

I nodded. "How's Julie taking it?"

He smiled reassuringly. "She's fine. Don't worry."

Photographers and reporters were waiting in the hall when we emerged. Crowds filled the hall and stairs, trying for a peek at a real, live murderer. Flashbulbs started popping all over the place. The reporters, some of whom I knew personally, fired a barrage of questions at me as we pushed and shoved our way toward the stairs. It was a bedlam. I kept shaking my head and repeating, "No comment. No comment."

Gainey and Wagner had a hectic time getting me downstairs through the mass of humanity, but we made it. I'd finally made the grade. I was a celebrity.

Later I was removed to the Hummock County jail by a couple of deputies. It seemed that in crimes involving a capital offense the county had jurisdiction over the prisoner. The facilities here were clean and modern. A carton of cigarettes and more magazines arrived. It was a little late, but Emmaline Royal was trying to make amends.

Tuesday morning I was taken to Judge Maitland's court where Jamieson was waiting for me. Wilbur Hooks was there, looking as pompous as ever, along with Lieutenant Gainey. Also present was the old man, Jennings, the teller from my bank and the two police officers I had met on Waterfront Street on Friday night.

Judge Maitland, looking quite distinguished under his thatch of snow-white hair, listened attentively while Hooks presented the state's reasons for denying me bail. Jennings testified to the struggle I'd had with the murdered man shortly before the slaying. The teller told about the money I'd withdrawn from the bank. He then identified the money found on Zack Tully's body as the same money he'd given me. The two officers definitely placed me in the murder area on the night Tully was killed. Gainey was last. He told how his investigation uncovered my association with Mrs. Royal, and how an anonymous tip had led him to the murder weapon.

When the state had presented its last witness, Jamieson told me to take the witness stand and tell my story.

I was glad there were no spectators gawking at me. My insides were jumping. I told everything as simply as I could. Nobody asked questions or interrupted me and, when I was through, Jamieson smiled and motioned me down.

Judge Maitland studied the papers on his desk before clearing his throat.

"After carefully considering the facts as presented by Wilbur Hooks, representing the State of Florida, and by Robert Jamieson, representing the accused, Neil Cowan," he said in a solemn voice. "I find it will not endanger the state's case if the accused, Neil Cowan, is released temporarily on bail. Therefore, if he, or anyone representing him, will post collateral in the amount of ten thousand dollars, I see no reason why he cannot be released."

I was free on bail, or would be, just as soon as an order could be signed and served on the Sheriff of Hummock County.

The writ came through Wednesday morning. I picked up my belongings and walked out of the building with Bob Jamieson.

"How do you feel?" he asked.

"Fine. Thanks for everything, Bob."

"Come on. I'll take you home." We went to his car and got in. I looked around, hoping to see Julie. She was nowhere in sight.

"Julie all right?" I asked anxiously.

"She was okay the last time I saw her," he said. "Aren't you interested in who put up your bail?"

"Mrs. Royal?"

He eased into the morning traffic and nodded. "I gave them her personal check," he said. "You know, Neil, she's not a bad skate."

I didn't say anything. I had loved Emmaline Royal, or had thought I did. But it was over, and my thoughts were on Julie and Linda. I wanted to see them so badly it hurt.

An unpleasant thought hit me. "The newspapers," I said. "I suppose they've been having a field day?"

"I'm afraid so. Your arrest came too late for the Sunday papers, but they've sure played it up since. Pictures and all."

I groaned. While I was in jail feeling sorry for myself, Julie had been going through a private hell of her own.

Bob let me out in front of the house. Maple Street seemed unusually quiet, and I had the eerie feeling that everyone in the neighborhood was glaring at me from behind curtains or blinds.

"Your car's in the garage, Neil," he said. "Try not to worry too much. I'll get in touch in the morning."

I thanked him again and went slowly up the walk to the front door. It was the longest thirty feet I'd ever walked. The door was locked and I opened it with my key. I figured Julie was shopping, but the house had a silent, unlived-in feeling. Fear gripped my stomach, and I hurried through the rooms. The house was empty.

Then I saw it, on my dresser. An envelope with my name scrawled across it in Julie's handwriting.

My hands were shaking as I opened it:

Dear Neil,

I'm going away with Linda. Please don't think too harshly of me, but everything has happened so fast that I need time to adjust and consider. Please don't try to find us. Believe me, it is better this way.

Julie

My eyes filled with tears and for the first time in years I wept.

CHAPTER FOURTEEN

It was dark when I finally snapped out of it. I was in the living room, slumped in an armchair. The house and the street outside were quiet. Julie's note lay on the floor at my feet. My arms were lumps of lead, and there was a sick feeling in my stomach. I had never felt worse in my life.

I managed, somehow, to push aside my lethargy and switch on some lights, fix a sandwich and coffee. I drank the coffee, but just looking at the sandwich almost gagged me, and I pushed it away.

The little fat man was dead. That left the man with the Spanish accent and the open window in John Royal's den as my only leads. It surprised me to learn that I could still think of clearing myself. But even so, it looked hopeless. I didn't know where to start. How do you go about looking for a man with a Spanish accent in a city of forty-five thousand people? As for the open window — that was the merest hunch. It might mean nothing.

I washed my dishes and put them away. I took a strip of waxed paper, covered the sandwich and put it in the refrigerator. Back in the living room, I avoided looking at the television set because it reminded me of Julie. The place wasn't the same without her and Linda. People and their problems make a home, not furniture, draperies and knick-knacks.

The phone rang and I picked up the receiver.

"Neil!" It was Emmaline. "I've been calling you all

afternoon. Are you all right?"

"Yes, I'm fine."

"When I couldn't get you, I called Mr. Jamieson. He said not to worry, that you'd probably gone somewhere."

"No. I was here."

"You sound strange, Neil. What's wrong?"

"She's left me, Emmaline."

"Oh, no!" There was a long, tragic pause. "I feel terrible, Neil. But maybe it's only temporary. She'll come back, you'll see."

"I hope so. Thanks for everything, Emmaline."

She was silent a moment. Then: "What are your plans?"

"There isn't much I can do," I said. "Jamieson says the state's attorney won't have any trouble getting an indictment. He figures I'll go on trial some time in early November."

"I'll help all I can, Neil. Will I see you soon?"

"In a day or two, perhaps. I'd like to get a little oriented first."

"Of course. Call me — please?"

"It's a promise," I said.

After I hung up, I took a hot shower and toweled off vigorously. It made me feel better, although nothing could salve the ache in my heart. Donning pajamas, I lay back on the living-room couch and tried to think. And then the heartache began to grow. In a few minutes, it completely took over. The feeling of physical well-being induced by the shower disappeared. I seemed to myself to be hollow, a shell, completely empty except for the lump of misery where my heart should have been. The hell with this, I thought. I couldn't stand it. I would break up.

I jumped from the couch and began to pace the room. I looked at my hands. They were shaking. I walked into the kitchen, flung open a cabinet, contemplated the bottle of vermouth standing there and, next to it, an almost full fifth of gin.

I never was much of a drinker. The liquor was on hand chiefly in the event that some dinner guest or other should want a martini. But now I seized the gin bottle as if it were the answer to my prayers. I poured a generous slug into a tumbler, diluted it with tap water, and tossed it down. I waited a few moments, then imbibed more of the same. Again I looked at my hands. They were not shaking.

Carrying bottle and glass, I returned to the living room, sat down on the couch, and proceeded to pour down more gin, neat.

As I have said, I am no drinker. Cocktails, occasionally. A brandy after dinner. A highball or two with a friend in a bar. But successive jolts of gin such as I was taking now were unprecedented. I felt a burning in my gullet, and a rosy warmth that seemed to spread outward from the pit of my stomach to my arms and legs. My head became lightly, pleasantly fogbound; my brain seemed permeated by a roseate mist. For the moment I could almost forget that disaster had overtaken my life. I poured another slug.

As I lifted the tumbler to my mouth, the door chimes chose to ring.

Who? I didn't try to guess. I couldn't care less. Unless . . . maybe Julie. Had Julie come home?

I set down the glassware on an end table and, staggering slightly, made for the door. I threw it open.

On the threshold stood Kathy, in one of those scant summer dresses, brightly yellow in the light of the foyer lamp.

"Oh," I said.

She looked at me. "You seem disappointed, Mr. Cowan."

"Oh, no. Not at all. Glad to see you, as a matter of fact. Come right in." I slammed the door shut. We marched into the living room. "Sit there," I said, indicating the couch. I sat down beside her and resumed lapping my alcohol. "Oh," I said. "I'm not being very polite, now, am I? Would you care for a drink, too?"

She was still looking at me, her gray eyes wide and innocent. After a couple of moments she said firmly, "Yes, I would like a drink."

I handed her my tumbler. She sipped, started to sputter.

"I can't get that down, Mr. Cowan," she said, as if ashamed of herself.

"Neil is the name, as you know very well. And just give me back that glass. I'll fix it for you."

Complete with stagger, I started for the kitchen. I made it handily, thinking to myself that I was going to be a lot more tolerant of drunkards in future. They had a point. I threw open the refrigerator, extracted ice and a bottle of orange soda, the kind Linda likes. I returned to the living room with these accessories, plus a second tumbler, and mixed my visitor something that must have been fairly palatable, for she drank it off at one gulp and asked for another. I obliged.

"Mr. Cowan — I mean Neil — I'm sorry Mrs. Cowan has left you. That's right, isn't it?" The girl looked around doubtfully. "She isn't here, is she?"

"No. How did you know about it?"

"She phoned the office. She said that if you showed up I should tell you to eat dinner out, because there wouldn't be any at home. She had been suddenly called away, she said. You weren't at the office, so I couldn't give you the message — but I guessed the rest. She doesn't want to be the wife of a murder suspect, is that it?"

I sipped gin. "That's it, Kathy. And you came to comfort me? Maybe cook my dinner? Very nice of you."

"Well, I don't believe you're any old murderer. Why, you wouldn't harm a fly." She sipped gin and orange soda. "But I came, really, because I'm following your advice. I'm here because I want to make Willie jealous. That's what you told me to do, isn't it?"

We were seated side by side on the couch. My head was spinning a trifle but I felt in good control of myself. A flush was taking possession of Kathy's fresh, young face. The alcohol, no doubt.

"Ah," I said. "Willie."

"Yes. We had a date for tonight. He came in his car to pick me up. But on impulse, I walked right past him, got into a cab, and came here. I saw him follow."

"Well, I suppose I might as well be hung for a philanderer as for a murderer." I laughed. "It will be good for his soul, all right. Is he outside now?"

"He drove off, once he learned my destination."

She pushed herself up from the couch, looked around in somewhat wild-eyed but hesitant fashion. Obviously, the liquor was bothering her. She took one cautious step away from me, halted, looked at me in mute appeal.

"That way," I said. "The door to the left of the stairway."

She walked off carefully, tottering only mildly, and after a minute or so returned looking more comfortable. Her slim legs poked out gawkily in front as she sat down on the couch again, a little closer to me, and courageously tossed off what was left in her glass. I stared at the legs. Nice legs, I thought. Why hadn't I ever noticed them before?

"So maybe I'm making Willie jealous," she said in her fresh, soft voice. "But Neil, is that really the answer? Will that cure him of his indifference? Will he stop holding me off and putting me off — standing me up and knocking me down? I doubt it. Oh, Neil. . . ." She choked up, and in a moment the tears were gushing. "Neil," she sobbed, "why can't he be like you? So kind and tolerant and — and wise!"

"There, there," I soothed. Her head had found my shoulder, and I stroked her toast-brown curls in what I hoped was comforting fashion. "He'll come around." In this position, the décolleté of the square-necked yellow dress was quite exaggerated, and I could not help viewing the rise and fall of her plump and creamy breasts, cradled in lacy nylon, as they rose and fell with her sobs. One of them came intimately into contact with my pajama-clad chest and I felt stirrings that had nothing to do with alcohol. Guiltily, I moved away from her a little, but she shifted her body, flung her arms around me. She was crying uncontrollably.

"Oh, Neil — Neil — what's wrong with me? You're a man. You must know. Why don't I really attract Willie?"

Now I stroked her bare, suntanned arm. How young she was, I thought. The feeling of her skin against my fingers, however, did nothing to calm my stirrings. Yes, I was a man. A man like any other. My body could not remain wholly indifferent to a pretty girl in my arms, a girl with the dew of adolescence still on her, a girl palpitating with the emotions and juices of warm nubility. "You attract him," I said, my tone nervously husky. "It's just that you don't hold him. So far as I know, he is healthy and male. He needs — well — Kathy, I'm going to talk to you as if you were my grown daughter. Your Willie needs satisfaction, of sorts. Do you give that to him? Do you live up to the promise your body makes to him, the promise which is the essence of attraction?"

She pushed herself away from me, shocked. The tears stopped.

"Neil, I'm not one of those easy girls. When I reach my marriage bed, I want to be undefiled. I want my husband to know I'm pure."

"Commendable, I'm sure. But it isn't a matter of all or nothing. As I suppose you are aware, lesser measures can be resorted to — measures permitting you to remain technically unsullied — "

"I don't know what you're talking about!"

In her outraged innocence, if that's what it was, she was blushing furiously and charmingly. Meanwhile, the yellow dress had pulled up well above her knees. I looked at the creamy thighs of her, and gulped.

"Kathy," I said severely, "don't you ever feel yearnings? Aren't you human?"

"I'm human, all right. I often have desires. But they're wrong, sinful, so I ignore them. I don't let them get the better of me. That's the way I was raised."

"Have boys ever kissed you?"

"On dates? Sure. By the time I got out of high school I had been thoroughly kissed on many occasions, especially in parked cars."

"Anything more?"

"Some of the boys tried. Hugs. Poking and pushing and fondling . . . and one or two got a lot further than that, before I put a stop to things. The whole bit disgusted me. Grunting, sweating, piggish males trying to glut themselves on me — "

"And Willie. He disgusts you too? When he wants you?"

"Well, no. I like him to want me. When he wants me, I feel myself wanting him too. But I won't let him spoil me and dirty me. He can have me, all of me, every inch of me — once we're married."

"But that's why he gives you trouble. Probably he has to go to other girls once in a while for relief. You should give him that relief, especially if you love him. You should help him."

She bit her lip. "To be honest, Neil, I think I would — if I knew how. I'm shy, Neil. I don't let him show me things, teach me — I'm so self-conscious about — about . . ."

"Come here, my dear," I said, meaning to be kind to

her — or at least that's what I told myself.

We had been speaking quite rationally. It did not seem that the gin had too much of a hold on us, even though only a couple of ounces were left in the bottle. Yet both of us must have been pretty drunk to allow ourselves to do what followed next. As she moved closer, obediently, she also swung her long, bare legs across my pajama-encased ones; whether her intentions were less than innocent or whether she was merely trying to make herself comfortable, I still don't know. But encouraged by her trustfulness, or her deliberate incitement, whichever it was, I placed my hands on her trim waist and lifted her to my lap.

"Want to know how to proceed?" I whispered into her coral ear. And I could not resist. I kissed it.

"Oh, yes, Neil. Yes!" She wriggled happily, settling her curves more snugly against me.

"Start this way, of course." I murmured, kissing her full on her soft red lips. "Then — "

No need for talk, after that.

I did not have courage to tamper with her clothing. But through the thin cotton of the dress I felt the warm tumult of her breasts, and I grasped them, one in each hand. Lovely ovals. Sweet fruits of womanhood, lushly rewarding, richly provocative. She gasped, then let me stroke them, fondle them. Then my hands strayed elsewhere, and I led her hands on their own explorations; the tickling, tenuous journeys of palm and finger were interrupted by gasps and sighs from each of us. What delight, I was thinking. And to silence my conscience I told it that I was helping her, that was all — educating her in womanhood as she needed to be educated.

For minutes thereafter we embraced and kissed and squirmed and fondled, going through the whole program of pleasures so often pursued by young couples before the solace of marriage is available to them. The result was inevitable. I knew I must not harm her, must not — God forgive me for thinking it — attack her. But I knew also that somehow I must find surcease. Besides, this was the point of the lesson, was it not?

She needed no urging. Willingly she disposed herself as I wished her to, bending her young, delightful body to my needs. My arms crushed her, my lips buried themselves in her sweet-smelling hair. I did not have to tell her how to move, where to move, any more than I had to tell myself. She was perfectly safe. Wisps of clothing remained between us, and there was no penetration. My agonized contortions abruptly ceased, and in this she recognized the crowning of my pleasure.

"Am I all right, Neil? Did you enjoy me?" Her gray eyes were sparkling in the lamplight.

"I enjoyed you," I said heavily.

"Oh, Neil, I'm glad. I'll remember this. I'll know how to — " She broke off abruptly, again a shy youngster. Her eyelids fell, masking the sparkle. She carefully arranged the wrinkled yellow dress, paying much attention to adequately draping breast, thigh and knee. But she was still breathing hard, I noticed. Her agitation would not still itself.

Now guilt came on me in a flood, and I think on her too. We both sprang to our feet at the same moment.

She kept her eyes raised, as if ashamed and afraid of viewing anything below chin level. I turned, fled to my bedroom closet, flung on a bathrobe, then hastily returned to her. She had the gin bottle to her lips, and was emptying it.

"Kathy!"

She set down the bottle. She took a step or two, reeling, and fell to the couch. I sought refuge in the kitchen, broke open the vermouth and, hoping to still the storm in me, drank of it as a man would drink water. When I returned to the living room, I was definitely besotted beyond control. Though I could not walk straight, talk straight, think straight, see straight, I lifted the vermouth bottle to my lips again, tossed off most of the rest of it — and fell to the couch.

Kathy was no longer lying there.

She was on her feet, staggering about the room before me in a grotesque caricature of dancing. She was humming a tune to herself, interrupting it with giggles and snaps of the fingers. As I watched in shocked, drunken stupor, she loosened the fastenings of the yellow dress, flung it to the rug. She followed this with bra and briefs. "Neil, look at me! Neil, aren't I beautiful? A girl to kiss? A girl to love?" She spun heavily, and fell on her face.

I crawled over to her.

"Kathy, you're drunk."

"Sure. We're both drunk. We're both lovely, lovely drunk." She giggled wildly, flung herself across me and kissed me. "Neil, what do you think I am? Wood? Stone? You did just as bad to me as you say I did to Willie. You picked me way up — then marooned me — "

She pulled apart the lapels of my robe, and proceeded to cover me from head to toe with wild, wet kisses.

Through the fog of alcohol, one thing penetrated. I wanted her. I wanted her at any price. She had tempted me too far.

There followed what could only be called an orgy. In a desperate and sympathetically shared assault on pleasure, we explored every possibility of touch and caress and kiss. How I feasted on the rosy charms of her. How I satiated myself with her creamy breasts, drank of her lips and her thighs. Madly I conquered, one by one, each satin curve and velvet cranny of her, and in rampant wantonness she reciprocated, feeding and fanning my fires, fondling me to passion so powerful it was pain.

And then our sweating bodies locked in the full flow of mating. The rhythm of the ages possessed us. On the wings of fiery delight we mounted to heaven beyond heaven, to joys beyond joy, there to shatter ourselves into a million kaleidoscopic shards of glorious color and unspeakable bliss.

Two minutes later, in each other's arms, we reposed on the floor unconscious. Two drunken slobs. . . .

I think it was she who awoke first. I am not sure. But one stirred, and awoke the other, and both of us sat up, staring first in shock and then in fright.

It was Kathy, being female, who rescued us from our numbness with her essential practicality.

"All right, Neil," she said, gently stroking my cheek. "Don't look so forlorn about it. It's done. We can't cry over spilt milk. We both have to go on living."

"Do we?" I thought of wife and child gone, of murder attributed to me, of this young and trusting girl now spoiled, violated.

"I know what you're thinking, Neil. But I always did want you. Now I've had you. I was terribly jealous of Mrs. Royal, did you know? Neil, how do I rate? Am I as good as she?"

I had to smile. "Not quite yet, child. But you will be. You'll be better than anybody."

"See? So it was all for the best. You started me off right, and I'll know how to hold Willie, now. You stripped that priggishness from me. I wish I could do something for you. Now that your wife has run away, would you want me to marry you? I'd rather marry you than Willie, anyway."

"Nonsense. Go back to him and be happy. You've already honored me with your greatest gift — the gift of your body. I'll never forget that. The memory will always be with me. It will solace and strengthen me, Kathy."

She stared at me a moment with her wide gray eyes. Then she nodded, and kissed me on the lips.

"I'd better get out of here before my reputation is thoroughly ruined," she said. She rose from the floor and swiftly dressed. When she came back from the bathroom, her toast curls neatly combed, she said, "Do you have a headache?"

"No."

"Either do I. No hangovers. That's a good sign. Well, goodbye, Neil."

She walked out into the gray dawn. I wasn't worried about her. The cabs start cruising early, in our town. I looked at the clock. Five-thirty. I stretched out on the couch and fell asleep again.

I awoke feeling refreshed. The day was bright, sunny. I showered, shaved and made breakfast, then left for the office.

Kathy gave me a little smile when I arrived. She was cold as ice. She acted as if nothing whatever had happened between us. "Welcome back, Mr. Cowan," she said.

"Thank you, Kathy. How's everything been going?"

"There've been a lot of calls," she said. She dropped her eyes. "But they weren't business. Reporters, photographers, writers and just plain crackpots."

I nodded and went into my office. There was a stack of messages on my desk and I thumbed through them fast. As Kathy said, none of them concerned real estate. I threw them in the waste basket.

A couple of calls came in during the morning. A man who said he was a writer wanted to do a byline story about my difficulties. I hung up on him. A sob sister for the Jellico *Sentinel* called, asking for an interview. I explained that my lawyer had advised me against making public statements until after the trial.

No business calls came in, but that didn't surprise me. The way I figured it, folks would stay clear of Neil Cowan until after the trial. I got to thinking about what Julie was using for money. She had some money of her own, but it would not last very long.

After Kathy went to lunch, I stood by the back window, thinking. I was wasting time, sitting around doing nothing. There had to be some angle I could check. I hadn't killed John Royal or Zack Tully, yet I was the number one candidate in both murders.

No matter which way my thoughts went, the man with the Spanish accent kept coming back. He was the crux of the whole case against me. He had tried to get me to Peacock Hill on the night John Royal was murdered, and had conned me into getting him the thousand dollars he had planted on Zack Tully's body. The first maneuver had left me without an alibi; the second had tied me to a murder.

I was still conjecturing when the phone rang. Bob Jamieson wanted to know how I felt and I told him I was coming around okay.

"You know about Julie?" I asked.

"Yes, Neil, and I'm sorry. Emmaline Royal called last night and told me. She wants to hire a private investigator to find her."

"Why, for God's sake?"

Bob hesitated a moment and then said, "She made me promise not to tell you, but I'm going to anyway. She wants to find Julie so that she can talk her into going back to you."

It was a nice gesture, a wonderful gesture. Or did it go beyond a mere gesture? The mistress who stuck by her lover while his wife deserted him.

I said, "I don't want it that way, Bob. I want Julie back in the worst way, but only if she wants to come back."

"I know, Neil. I told Emmaline you'd feel that way."

"Thanks."

"The grand jury meets a week from today," Jamieson said. "I'm positive that Hooks has enough to get an indictment. That means your bail will be recalled."

"And I go back to jail?"

"Only temporarily, I hope," he said. "We'll have to go before Judge Maitland again. Maitland's a pretty good guy most of the time, but he's got one habit. He seldom grants bail once a grand jury indicts."

Which meant I had only a week to break two murders, I thought. A feeling of urgency possessed me. I wanted to run helter-skelter, ferreting out the truth—only I didn't know where to begin.

I promised Bob to be in his office Saturday morning for a conference. He wanted my entire story down on paper so that he could have something to go on.

I lit a cigarette and wondered where to start. There was no use bothering Emmaline. But how about Riley Martin? He had produced a reliable witness for his whereabouts at the time of the murder, but reliable witnesses had been bought before.

I remembered that Martin was a golf enthusiast. I phoned the Jellico Country Club and learned that he had a two o'clock reservation.

When Kathy returned from lunch, I headed for Peacock Hill. The possibility that Martin was involved in some way with John Royal's murder seemed remote, but I had to begin somewhere and it was about time I got lucky.

I got lucky.

There was a parking lot at the intersection of Belvedere Drive and Arrowwood Road. I decided to wait for him there. I drove in. An overalled attendant sauntered over and started to put a tag on my windshield wiper.

"I'm waiting for a friend, so that won't be necessary,"

I told him. I gave him a dollar. "This should cover it."

He nodded, pocketed the dollar and went back to his little four-by-five shack to get out of the sun. I didn't blame him — the day was hot. I removed my coat. My wrist watch said 1:15.

I had just lit a cigarette and settled back when I saw Martin's Porsche coming down the hill. I waited until he turned left at the intersection before sliding into the traffic behind him. Tailing the red sports car was like following a fire engine. I was able to keep a discreet distance behind.

But he surprised me. Instead of following Belvedere Drive to the Country Club Road, he swung left onto Overbrook Drive. It wasn't the way to the golf course, and my pulse quickened. Several blocks later he made another left turn onto Planters Street. There were still several cars between us.

Planters Street was a lower-than-middle-class section composed of rooming houses, a few hotels and more than a few taverns. He parked before one called the Magic Lantern and went in. I found an empty spot a short distance away and cut the engine. It was 1:30.

His stopping here puzzled me. If he'd wanted a drink, the country club had the best liquor in the county, and from what I'd heard, Riley Martin always traveled first class. I waited and wondered.

He came out after a few minutes, got in the car and made a right turn at the first intersection. I followed. When he came again to Overbrook Drive, he swung left. I let a beat-up Chevy and a Ford pickup get between us before I took after him. This time he was headed in the right direction for the golf course. A few minutes later he turned into the winding driveway that leads to the fieldstone clubhouse. I kept on going.

I drove to the Magic Lantern.

The bar was crowded, but I found an empty stool at the far end and ordered bourbon and water. The clientele was noisy. There was a telephone booth a few feet from where I sat. The first time the man with the Spanish accent called I had heard voices and jukebox music. A television set stood near the other end of the bar and I saw a small, back-bar radio, but there wasn't a jukebox in sight.

Disappointed, I finished my drink and went back to the office. Kathy was reading the inevitable movie magazine.

She looked up. "You had a call a little while ago," she said. "But the man hung up when I told him you weren't in."

"Did he say what he wanted?"

"No. I could hardly understand him, he had such a foreign accent."

"Can you remember exactly what time he called?"

Kathy frowned. "Let me see. It was around one-thirty, give or take a minute."

I went to my desk, my heart pounding. There was no doubt about it. Riley Martin was the man with the Spanish accent! It explained a lot of things and yet it explained nothing as far as getting myself cleared with the police was concerned. Because there was one great big hitch. I couldn't prove it.

I'd heard a jukebox when he had made his first call, yet there was no such machine in the Magic Lantern.

That didn't mean anything, for he could have called from any number of spots. Acting on impulse, I checked the number of the Magic Lantern in the telephone book and dialed it. A gruff-voiced female answered I could hear a hub-bub of voices in the background.

"Could I speak to the bartender, please?" I asked.

"Just a minute."

I waited almost five minutes. Then a voice said, "Mike Spivey."

"Mike, do you have a jukebox in your place?"

"We did, but some crazy jerk broke it the other night. We're waitin' for a new one. Why, you want to put one in?"

I assured him that I didn't, thanked him and hung up. He probably thought I was nuts.

An idea came to me and I called Kathy. When she walked in I handed her my car keys. "Drive over to the *Sentinel* building and pick up a copy of Riley Martin's picture from the photo library," I said. I gave her five dollars to pay for it.

She took the keys and the money and left. I walked around the office, smoking and wondering about what I had just learned. Just knowing that Riley Martin was the man with the Spanish accent opened the door to many possibilities. Among them was that he had, somehow, masterminded the murder of John Royal. I wondered if Emmaline knew, or even suspected, that her brother had killed her husband.

Kathy returned with an eight-by-ten photograph of Riley Martin and two dollars in change. The face that smiled up at me was an excellent likeness, the photo must have been taken recently.

I told Kathy to close the office at four. Then I got in the car and headed for Corry Heights, where the late Zack Tully had lived.

There was no Tully in the Corry Heights telephone directory, so I started asking questions around town. For a man with Tully's background, the poolrooms and taverns seemed like the best place to start. After about the fifth inquiry, I got an address on Amby Street. I drove there and found it to be a small white bungalow.

A neat bed of periwinkles graced the front lawn and the Bermuda grass was freshly cut. I rang the bell and waited. The rattan furniture on the porch looked old. A short, pleasant-faced woman in her fifties came to the screen door. She was wearing black. She didn't say anything, just looked at me with sad eyes.

I took off my hat. "Mrs. Tully?"

She nodded. "I've seen you some place," she said. "What do you want?"

I took Riley Martin's picture from my pocket and showed it to her. "Did you ever see this man before?" I asked.

"What are you, a cop?"

"No, ma'am."

"Then who are you? Give me a name."

"Fred Green," I lied. "About the pictures, ma'am?"

She looked at the picture and then at me. "No, I've never seen him before," she said. "Why?"

I ignored her question. "Do you have a telephone?"

She nodded. She was still studying my face. "It's unlisted."

"Did a man with a Spanish accent ever call your

husband?"

I was swinging wildly, but her eyes registered surprise. I had hit paydirt! "How did you know?" she asked.

Suddenly her eyes registered something else. Hate. She had recognized me. "I know who you are!" she cried. "You're Neil Cowan, the man who murdered my husband! Murderer! Murderer!"

I could tell by the look in her eyes that she wasn't going to be placated, so I turned and hurried towards the car.

The screen door banged behind me. "Murderer! Murderer!" she screamed. She was following me. People were beginning to stick their heads out of windows.

I got out of the neighborhood fast. She was still screaming and waving her arms when I last saw her in the rearview mirror.

It was after five when I reached the outskirts of Jellico, and stopped in a diner for something to eat. But I was wound too tight to enjoy the food. Riley Martin had purchased the gun that killed John Royal and Zack Tully from the little fat man himself. I could be off the hook in a hurry if I could prove it.

I drove into my garage a little past six. I locked the doors, went into the house. The familiar rooms were deserted and lonely and I felt depressed. I decided not to stay another night. I boiled some fresh coffee and had a cup. There was a restlessness in me that wouldn't be stilled. I finished the coffee, lit a cigarette and roamed aimlessly from room to room.

Everything I saw reminded me of Julie and Linda,

and I wondered where they were and what they were doing. The ache in my heart told me how much I missed them. I wandered to the big picture window in the living room and peered out between the blinds.

A trio of youngsters about Linda's age was playing across the street, wearing cowboy suits. Two were facing each other, legs spread in the typical let's-see-who's-faster scene. They both drew on cue and the farthest boy in the driveway clutched his stomach and staggered to the ground in the familiar style of TV Westerns. The victorious gunman then hurried to the sidewalk where he encountered his second adversary. This time the ambidextrous youngster went for the pistol on his left hip, and again he triumphed.

Something about the scene I had just witnessed nudged at my brain. It had been enacted by comparative babies, yet there was something in the two scenes that bothered me. I went over them again in my mind, picturing them just as I had seen them. The solution was there, somewhere, if I could only find it.

And then it hit me. The pieces of the puzzle suddenly fell into place.

I knew who had killed John Royal.

And I knew how it had been done.

CHAPTER FIFTEEN

It was the moment of truth, and the knowledge staggered me. I had all the answers now, or most of them, and the whole thing was so absurdly simple that I could hardly believe it.

I knew something else, too. Lois Bowman's father had not committed suicide. Like John Royal, he had been murdered. And the open windows in both murders were no coincidence but an integral part of a fiendishly clever plan.

My insides were churning as I turned away from the window. There were a couple of points still to be cleared up before Lieutenant Gainey would be completely satisfied. I considered calling Bob Jamieson and asking his advice, but vetoed the idea. Call it egotism or a desire for personal revenge, but whatever it was, I had been made a fool of, had been clobbered, humiliated and branded a murderer before all my friends. Even worse, I had lost my wife, my child and my home.

This was my time to crow.

I was moving toward the telephone when it rang. I picked it up. It was Bob Jamieson and he sounded excited.

"Neil, I'm glad I got you! Lois Bowman just called me."

"Where is she?" I asked.

"I don't know, but it was an out-of-town call. She read about my being your lawyer, and she's coming to

Jellico to talk to me."

"She's still in danger, Bob."

"I tried to warn her, but she was adamant. She says she hasn't enough evidence to get you off the hook, but what she knows will make Gainey do some thinking."

If she was already on her way, there was nothing I could do or say to stop her. But she was in danger if certain people saw her before she got to Jamieson.

"You still there, Neil?"

"I'm still here," I said. "Did she say why she left Jellico?"

"Yes. She said a man with a Spanish accent called her on the phone and threatened her. She became frightened. Think it could be the same one who called you?"

"I'm sure of it. Will you be home all evening?"

"Yes. Why?"

"I'll call you later if everything goes okay."

"Neil —"

I hung up on him.

Dusk was falling when I backed the car out of the driveway. Carl Peterson was mowing his front lawn and he smiled uncertainly at me and waved. I waved back and headed for Arrowwood Road and the home of Mr. and Mrs. Sam Proctor. Their house was several hundred feet from the Royal mansion and was partially screened from the street by a ten-foot hedge. There were no other cars in sight when I drove into the driveway and cut the engine.

The Proctor home was not as pretentious as the house of death up the street, nor was it as new. It was a stately, colonial-style pile with imposing white columns and an open porch that extended its width. The lawn and shrubbery showed signs of neglect, and there was an air of faded glory about the place as I went up on the porch and worked the heavy, old-fashioned knocker. From where I stood I could see the darkened upper floor of the Royal home.

After several minutes, a porch light came on. Mrs. Proctor, wearing a chenille robe, peered out at me.

Before I could say anything, she asked, "You're Neil Cowan, aren't you?"

"Yes."

"What do you want?"

"Your help, if you'll give it to me."

She stood for several moments, trying to make up her mind. Then she unlatched the screen door and said, "Come in."

I followed her through the spacious hall. The house had a musty smell, as if the windows hadn't been open in years. In the dim light I could see a winding stairway leading upstairs. The furniture was outdated but well preserved. I followed her into a room on the right and she closed the sliding doors behind us.

Mrs. Proctor gestured me to a chair. She chose a wooden rocker. When she was comfortable, she fixed her beady eyes on me.

"What do you want, young man?" she asked.

I knew that, despite her age, she was sharp as a tack and decided an honest approach would be the best.

"At the inquest," I said, "you testified that Mrs. Royal was some distance away when you and your husband heard the shot."

She nodded. "That's right. What about it?"

"Can you recall exactly where Mrs. Royal was standing at the time?"

"Of course," she replied impatiently. "I may be old, but I'm not blind."

"Would you tell me where she was standing?"

"Do you know anything about trees, young man?"

"A little."

"There is a *Plantanus occidentalis* up the street a-ways," she said. "It's the only one on the street, so you can't miss it. She was standing next to it when Mr. Royal was shot."

I grinned sheepishly. "What's a *Plantanus occidentalis?*"

"A sycamore, young man."

I nodded gratefully. "One more question. Was Mrs. Royal carrying a handbag that night?"

"She was."

I picked up my hat and rose. "Thank you, Mrs. Proctor," I said. "You've been most kind."

She paid no attention to me and kept on rocking. "Speaking of that handbag reminds me of something," she said thoughtfully. "Mrs. Royal never once laid it aside. Not even when she was kneeling by her dead husband's body. Was she concealing something in it, young man?"

She was sharp, all right. "I think so," I said, moving towards the hall.

She followed me to the front door. She was latching the screen door when she asked, "You really didn't kill Mr. Royal, did you?"

"No, ma'am, I didn't."

"Or that Mr. Tully, either?"

"No."

She smiled at me for the first time. "I didn't think you did."

I left my car in the driveway and went up the street. The sycamore was approximately a hundred feet from the Royal property. I took out my pencil flashlight and played the beam around the base of the tree. After more than five minutes I had drawn a blank. What I was looking for was not there. Then I started playing the light around the trunk. I worked up slowly, praying that I would find what I came for. It had to be here, for my story to carry any weight. Without it, I would only have my word against a couple of million dollars.

And then I found it.

It was high up on the trunk, near where the branches begin. It was barely discernible, even when I focused the light directly on it. But it would be all I needed to convince Lieutenant Gainey.

I hurried back to the car and drove to the drug store at the intersection of Arrowwood Road and Belvedere Drive. From a booth I telephoned police headquarters and asked for Lieutenant Gainey. The officer at the switchboard turned me over to the detective division.

"Wagner here."

"This is Neil Cowan, Sergeant," I said. "Let me speak to the lieutenant."

"He left about ten minutes ago."

"Can you get in touch with him? It's important."

"I'm not sure," Wagner said. "Can't it wait until morning?"

"I'm afraid not. I'm on my way to see Mrs. Royal. I've just found out who killed her husband."

"Who?"

"I'd prefer telling it to Lieutenant Gainey."

"Is this on the level, Cowan?" He sounded skeptical. "If it isn't, the lieutenant will have your hide."

"It's on the level, Sergeant. With a little luck, we'll bust this case wide open tonight."

"Okay, I'll see what I can do," Wagner said.

"See you there," I said, hanging up.

Next, I dialed the Royal residence. After nearly a dozen rings a maid picked up the receiver. I asked for Mrs. Royal.

"This is Neil, Emmaline," I said. "May I come to see you right away?"

"Of course! Where are you?"

"I'm calling from a phone booth at the foot of Arrowwood Road."

"Wonderful! Come on up, Neil, and hurry!"

I drove up to Peacock Hill again and turned into the Royal driveway. The second floor was still dark, but several rooms on the ground floor were lighted. I wondered if Riley Martin was hanging around somewhere. Emmaline let me in. She wore a skin-tight creation of clinging green silk. The woman on Peacock Hill, I thought. She even walked like one, beautiful and proud.

She took me to the big room overlooking the terrace where I had first met John Cameron Royal. She closed the door behind us and leaned against it. Her eyes were so filled with the joy of seeing me again that I wondered, even then, if I could be wrong.

She came to me and kissed me tenderly on the lips. "I'm glad you're here, Neil," she said.

And she meant it. That was the astonishing part.

There must have been something about the look in my eyes or the tautness of my body that warned her. She drew back with a puzzled frown.

"What's wrong, Neil?"

I shook my head. "It won't work for us, ever, Emmaline. You see, I finally know everything."

"You're not making sense. What do you know?"

"I know how John Royal was killed and who killed him. And that's not all, I know how James Joseph Bowman died, too."

If I expected her to crumble at my words, I was disappointed. She looked at me, bewilderment clouding her eyes.

"You must be tired and confused, Neil," she said, clutching my arm. "Please sit down and rest."

I shook her arm off. "I'm not tired and I'm not confused," I said. "In fact, I'm beginning to understand things for the first time in weeks." I shook my head in admiration. "You're a more amazing woman than I thought, Emmaline."

"Really, Neil — "

I watched her as she walked across the room and dropped into the big leather couch. She was a murderess, but still the loveliest creature I had ever seen.

"The moment you saw me that first day you knew you had me hooked," I said bitterly. "You were tired of the old man, or maybe he was getting fed up with you. Either way, you knew you had to do something and do it fast if you were to continue this way of life. I came along at exactly the right time. And I turned out to be the perfect patsy, because I fell for you like a ton of bricks."

She shook her head, incredulity still in her eyes.

"But a murder has to be perfectly planned to be successful," I said. "Or did you figure to do it a little differently from the Bowman murder? With him you made it look like suicide — and had everyone fooled except his daughter, Lois."

I saw surprise flash through her eyes and laughed.

"Yes, I've met her. She doesn't know how you managed to kill her father and get away with it, but I do. It was the open window — you shouldn't have repeated that. It's what the police call modus operandi — the weakest point in any criminal's armor."

She started to get up and leave the room, but I intercepted her, blocking her way. We stood inches apart and stared at each other, our eyes holding interminably. Suddenly, she closed her eyes, put her arms around my neck and kissed me. Her body went flat against mine and I could feel the pounding of my heart. Her perfume made my head swim, but this time I kept my senses despite my rising desire. Too much had happened since I had last succumbed.

I pushed her away from me, and she staggered backward onto the couch.

I said harshly, "I don't like to be used. Sucker is a dirty, ugly word."

She swallowed with difficulty, her eyes never leaving mine. "You fool!" she cried. "I wasn't even in the house when John was killed."

"You're right," I said. I was shaking with excitement, part of me wanting her — the rest of me revolted. "But John Royal was already dead when you went out to mail that letter. You killed him, but not before you made sure that all the windows in the den were closed. Why? Because it is a soundproof room, and you knew that the sound of the shot would not be heard outside the house. But once he was dead, you had to open one of the windows so that the sound of the second shot could be explained."

She pushed herself against the cushions, her hands braced on either side of her. There was a wild, desperate look in her eyes.

"That second shot was the real masterpiece," I said, shaking my head. "You knew that the Proctors took a walk every night before going to bed. They would make excellent witnesses because they were old and could easily be fooled into thinking that the shot had come from the house. You fired into the bole of that tree while the Proctors were some distance away and had their backs to you. That's why you took your handbag with you that night although you were only going to your mail box. You had a gun in it."

Her face was chalk-white, and she had trouble breathing. "But they heard the shot," she said hoarsely. "They said it came from the house."

"Yes, they heard the shot," I agreed. "But it was you who screamed and planted the idea in their heads that the shot had come from the house!"

"Neil, please — "

"And that trick of getting me where I would have no

alibi for the time of the murder was good, too. You set me up beautifully by being seen publicly with me. That was so Gainey wouldn't have any trouble picking up my trail. It was a masterpiece of planning right down the line." My hands were sticky with sweat and I wiped them against my coat. "There's only one thing I haven't got straight. Did you use the same gun that killed Royal to fire into the bole of the tree?"

"She used two guns."

I whirled. Riley Martin was standing by the door. There was a gun in his right hand and it was pointed at my middle.

The smile on my face was frozen. "Well, well," I said. "If it isn't Señor Raúl Antonio Lopez."

Riley Martin was a cool cat, I'll say that for him. He bowed from the waist, a mocking smile on his dark, handsome face.

He turned and looked at his sister with vicious eyes. "I told you my way was best," he said harshly. "But no, you wouldn't listen!"

I had pulled a boner that could cost me my life. In my excitement I had forgotten to consider that Martin might take me off guard. Since I knew their little secret, it was a cinch they weren't going to let me leave alive.

I took a deep breath. "May I ask a question, Señor Lopez?" I said.

"Go ahead."

"Why did you want me up here the night John Royal was killed? Was it because you had one plan and your sister another?"

Martin smiled. "I don't mind telling you now," he

said. His vigilance never slackened as he leaned against the door jamb. "The way I had it figured, we would kill Royal and then shoot you when you tried to escape. That way there would be no witnesses. It would simply be our word, and a few million dollars is hard to doubt."

"It might have worked," I said. I was stalling, hoping that Lieutenant Gainey would arrive in time. "What would my motive have been?"

Martin shrugged. "The same as it is now. He found out about you and Emmaline and called you on the carpet You got into an argument and shot him. I heard the shot, ran after you and shot you when you wouldn't stop."

"In the back?"

He shrugged again. "What's the difference? Back or front, you'd still be dead."

"Not bad," I said. "Why didn't you do it your way?"

He looked disdainfully at his sister. "Because she didn't want to see me kill you," he said. "Oh, don't get any wrong ideas about Emmaline. She didn't care if the state did it."

"How touching," I said.

Emmaline finally spoke, "What are we going to do, Riley?"

"We're going to get rid of him before he talks to Gainey," he said in a low, flat voice. "Then we're going to remove that slug from the tree. We should have done it before now. Fortunately, it's not too late."

"I'm afraid it is," I said. "I've already notified the police. They should be here any minute."

Riley grinned. "That won't do, Cowan," he said.

"You've seen too many movies."

"That gun," I said, pointing to it. "It makes you feel ten feet tall, doesn't it? You've been needling me ever since I first came up here. Put the gun away and let's see how tough you really are."

He threw back his head and laughed. "That won't do either." He gestured. "We're going through those french doors to your car. Make one funny move and I'll put a bullet in you."

He meant it. I don't think I was ever closer to death than I was at that moment.

I was moving towards the french windows when Emmaline asked, "Where are you going to do it?"

"Out in the woods somewhere," Martin said impatiently. "I'll make it look like suicide — if they ever find him. He's got plenty of reasons to knock himself off — disgrace, loss of family, all like that. And by the time he's found, we will be long gone. I've already started moving John's fortune abroad."

He was right. I had reasons to kill myself. But most of them concerned Julie and Linda, and thinking of them gave me a new surge of hope. I had to live at least long enough to clear myself. I whirled and threw myself at his legs in a football block. The gun went off almost in my ear and powder burn stung my eyes. But I wasn't hit. Martin fell on top of me and we rolled on the floor in a tangled heap.

I grabbed his gun hand, only to discover that the pistol had been knocked from his grasp by my lunge. He was heavier and in better condition, but I had one big item going for me, the desire to live. I was striking out blindly, hoping to get an advantage. Once I felt my fist hitting his jaw, but it was only a glancing blow and did little damage. His head moved away from another aimed at his jaw. He pulled me toward him with one hand and hit me in the stomach with the other. I tasted bile in my throat. He was as strong as an ox, and I figured the longer it took me to get him, the better his chances became.

We became untangled and he came charging at me. I tried to sidestep and kick his legs from under him in the same motion. I did neither. We fell onto the couch, grappling for an opening. He threw a left hook that caught me under the ear, making my head ring. I swung at his jaw and caught him hard enough for his eyes to unfocus.

It was the break I was looking for. He was hurt and briefly fighting by instinct. I tried to break loose and fight him at a distance, but he wouldn't have it. He charged again, butting his head into my stomach. We fell backward, knocking over an end table and a small lamp. I swung again, and he caught my left wrist, pulling me forward for a pile-driving left into my mid-section. The blow almost finished me, and I gasped for air.

A smile flickered across his face. He figured he had me, and I thought so, too. I could hardly breathe. But the knowledge of what lay ahead, if he won, kept me going. He moved in confidently, hooking a left to my head and bringing up a roundhouse right. I'd done enough boxing as a kid and in the army to expect this sucker maneuver, and slid easily inside the right. At the same time I brought up both fists with all my strength. It was an unorthodox punch, but it landed under his chin with such force that his head popped back. A glazed look came into his eyes as he staggered back.

I moved in after him. I measured him carefully and took aim with a short right that caught him smack on the button. He went over backward, turning a complete somersault. His eyes were open and he tried to get up, but his arms and legs wouldn't function. He couldn't make it. He was through.

My chest was heaving as I turned to look for the gun. I found it, all right. It was in Emmaline's hand and it was aimed at me.

"Emmaline," I said hoarsely. "Don't!"

Her face was twisted and her eyes were two chips of marble. The peacock had turned into a tigress.

"Riley was right," she said. "We should have done it his way. Maybe it isn't too late."

I held my hands up in front of me and backed away. I stared at her trigger finger in fascination. At any moment I expected a bullet to come crashing into my body. This is it, I told myself. And the funny part was, I wasn't thinking of myself. I was thinking of Julie and little Linda, and the lies they would be told when it was all over.

Her trigger finger whitened, and her eyes were narrow slits of hate. This was the woman for whom I had been going to sacrifice everything.

There was a noise somewhere in the house. Hoping it would distract her I jumped sideways. But I wasn't fast enough. There was a blinding flash and I could feel myself falling into a deep, dark abyss. I was turning over and over, and the last thing I remembered I was screaming my way into my own private hell.

CHAPTER SIXTEEN

When I opened my eyes, a face was peering down at me. It was Lieutenant Gainey. He looked the same as always.

"How do you feel, Cowan?" he asked.

"Okay, I guess," I said. I felt my head. There was a small bandage on my left forehead. "That's all there is?"

He nodded. "That's all. You were very lucky. She fired a second time, but missed. We stopped her before she could pull the trigger a third time."

"Thank God," I said. I couldn't believe it. I was lying on the leather couch and swung my feet to the floor. Except for a momentary dizziness and a slight headache, I didn't feel too bad.

I looked around. The room was empty.

"They're all down at headquarters," he said, divining my thoughts. "You took a chance coming up here by yourself."

"You know everything?"

He gave me a cigarette, took one himself and put a match to both. "Yes," he said, nodding. "Mrs. Royal broke down and told us the whole story. She even admitted shooting James Bowman three years ago. She seemed glad to tell it."

"You know about the bullet in the tree?" I asked.

"That, too. Sergeant Foster recovered it."

I shook my head. "It was quite a scheme."

"It was almost perfect, except for the open window,"

Gainey said. "How did you figure it out?"

I told him about the kids playing across the street from my house, and how the idea came to me while I was watching them.

He shook his head. "It was quite a gimmick," he said. "Of course the window puzzled us, but I doubt if we'd have ever figured it out."

"I was lucky."

He looked around at the disordered room. "I wish I could have seen the scrap," he grinned. "It must have been a beaut."

It was raining as we drove downtown in a police car. Bob Jamieson was waiting for us in Gainey's office. He had a big grin on his homely face.

"You crazy fool! You don't need a lawyer — you need a keeper." He shook my hand. "But I'm glad to see you're alive."

"That was the main idea," I said.

Gainey tossed his hat on the desk and waved us to chairs "You've had a rough night, Mr. Cowan," he said. "But if you're up to it, I'd like to get your deposition."

I agreed and he sent for Benny. After Benny left with my statement, Gainey explained that Riley Martin had murdered Zack Tully to protect himself against the murder weapon's being traced to him.

"Why was Tully following me?" I asked.

Gainey gazed at his cigarette thoughtfully. "Of course, I'm only guessing, but I think he wanted to warn you," he said. "He'd sold plenty of unregistered guns before, it was his business, but when he learned that Royal had been shot so soon after Martin bought two of his guns, he knew he was after something hot.

He did some checking, and picked up your trail.'"

"Why didn't he get in touch with me openly?"

"I'm still only guessing, but evidently he wasn't sure which side of the fence you were on," Gainey said. "You could have been in league with Martin. If you were and he tipped his hand to you, he'd be signing his own death warrant."

"Poor guy," I said.

"Don't feel sorry for the Zack Tullys of this world, Cowan," Gainey said harshly. "He's sold guns that have been used in stickups and murders all over the state. We're better off without his kind."

I turned to Jamieson. "Has Lois Bowman shown up yet?" I asked.

He nodded. "She got to my place about an hour after I called you," he said. "She's already told her story to the police."

I got to my feet. "I wonder what was in that envelope she gave me," I said thoughtfully. "Did she say?"

Jamieson stood up and Gainey followed suit "Yes, she told me," said Jamieson. "It was a marriage certificate."

"A marriage certificate? What makes that so important?"

Gainey smiled. "It wasn't an ordinary certificate, Mr. Cowan. You see, Emmaline and Riley Martin aren't brother and sister. They're husband and wife."

I had to sit down for that one. "No wonder the guy wanted to knock my brains out," I said, shaking my head.

Gainey and Jamieson laughed. I got up and was at the door when Gainey stopped me. He stuck out his hand.

"No hard feelings," he said. It was not a question or an apology, but a simple statement of fact. I shook hands with him and he added, "Your car is out back. I had one of the boys bring it in."

I thanked him and went into the hall with Jamieson. Some people came out of an adjoining room — two men and a woman. The men were detectives and the woman was Emmaline Royal.

She stopped when she saw me and for a brief moment she gave me that small smile I knew so well. She didn't say anything, just looked at me. One of the detectives prodded her and she went past me, her head erect, her step firm — still the most beautiful woman I had known.

Jamieson and I went down the wooden stirs. "My car is out front," Bob said. "I'll be seeing you around. Good luck, Neil."

He clasped my hand firmly and was gone.

I went out. The air was fresh and clean and, except for the heaviness still in my heart, I felt good.

I looked around for my car, saw it, and there were two people in the front seat.

Julie and Linda. I broke into a run. When I opened the car door, my eyes were wet and Julie's were very bright.

Linda said, "Mommy and I took a trip. It was fun, but I'm glad to be back."

"I'm glad to be back, too." I said.

A few days later, in the office, Kathy told me that she and her Willie were to be married in a month. She also confided that if she was to have a baby, it would not be mine.

I gave her a nice wedding present.

The End

Made in the USA
Columbia, SC
07 July 2024

38180412R00113